Kevin Laffan was born in Reading, Berks. He now lives in Wimbledon where the touring production of his West End play THE BEST PAIR OF LEGS IN THE BUSINESS was banned. He won the Dublin Festival Theatre Award for his play THE SUPERANNUATED MAN and the National Union of Students and Sunday Times Best Play Award for ZOO ZOO WIDDERSHINS ZOO (featured at the Edinburgh Festival with Lynn Redgrave). His first play for Television CUT IN EBONY, received an Award but was never produced; a comedy about racism in the USA, it was thought too controversial.

His many plays for television include - LUCKY FOR SOME (Jimmy Jewel) THE BEST PAIR OF LEGS IN THE BUSINESS (Reg Varney) DECISION TO BURN (Anthony Hopkins) FLY ON THE WALL (Trilogy, Julie Foster and Clive Francis) YOU CAN ONLY BUY ONCE etc.

He wrote BUD a series for Bud Flanagan, was lead writer for KATE, a series for Phyllis Calvert and I THOUGHT YOU'D GONE (with Peter Jones). He also created the long running series BERYL'S LOT and EMMERDALE.

His numerous plays for fringe theatres include; ADAM REDUNDANT, THERE ARE HUMANS AT THE BOTTOM OF MY GARDEN, ANGIE AND ERNIE (with Peter Jones), THE MISSIONARY AND OTHER POSITIONS, NEVER SO GOOD, THE CHILDREN OF CAIN, etc.

VIRGINS ARE IN SHORT SUPPLY

Kevin Laffan

Virgins are in Short Supply

PEGASUS
Elliot MacKenzie

PAPERBACK

© Copyright 2001
Kevin Laffan

The right of Kevin Laffan to be identified as author of
this work has been asserted by him in accordance with the
Copyright, Designs and Patents Act 1988

All Rights Reserved

No reproduction, copy or transmission of this publication
may be made without written permission.
No paragraph of this publication may be reproduced,
copied or transmitted save with the
written permission or in accordance
with the provisions of the Copyright Act 1956 (as amended).

Any person who does any unauthorised act in relation to
this publication may be liable to criminal
prosecution and civil claims for damage.

A CIP catalogue record for this title is
available from the British Library

ISBN 1 903490 05 7

First Published in 2001

**Pegasus Elliot Mackenzie Publishers Ltd.
Sheraton House Castle Park
Cambridge England**

www.pegasuspublishers.com

Printed & Bound in Great Britain

ACKNOWLEDGEMENTS

Thanks to Paul who made me

DEDICATIONS

JEANNE MY LOVE

PROLOGUE

Where Virgins Fear to Tread

"From time immemorial," said Sir Archibald, "the Humps were where local maids surrendered their virginity; now it usually happens on the back seat of a car."

"Less romantic but more convenient, I suppose."

"More uncomfortable I'd have thought, but strangers have been poking around on the Humps and Ackers is sure something funny is going on."

"Such as what?"

"I can't find out. I've asked around but nobody seems to know anything, which naturally makes me suspicious."

"Ask Tewson," said Judge Killearn. "He ought to know."

"Tewson? Good grief, there's no hope of the truth from him! He'd lie in his teeth to save a scratch to his skin. But then, a politician! What else can you expect?"

The judge sighed, exhaled blue cigar smoke and watched it rise towards the high ceiling of the members' bar. He shared his old friend's contempt for politicians in general and the reigning government in particular. Earlier in the day he had been compelled by the letter of a recent law to allow the eviction of a single mother and her two children from a council flat. Not for the first time in his judicial career he felt morally sick.

"Archie," he said. "At the end of this term I retire. We're both widowers. Why don't we get out of this country? Find somewhere more gentlemanly to live out what time's left to us."

"Where?"

"I fancy Italy. They seem to get on without a government most of the time."

"I'm tempted," said Sir Archibald. "There's nothing really to keep me here. I don't think Paula's ever going to marry. But I must find out what's happening to the Humps first. They used to belong to the family and I'm not having them ruined if I can help it."

"It's where those special newts are, isn't it?"

Sir Archibald nodded, "The red-speckled warty, very rare. Shelagh Breagh looks after them for some society or other. Nice girl."

"Get 'em made into a Site of Special Scientific Interest," said the judge.

CHAPTER ONE

She Who's Not Available…Meets the King of the One-night Stands

At Maggie Williams' party Shelagh Breagh was in conversation with Jimmy Williams about the state of religion when Pat Pendle butted in.

"If the beginning was a word," he said, "then it was probably an obscene one."

Shelagh bristled. "I don't think that's very funny."

"It's not meant to be. It's tragic. Look around!" Pat made a sweeping gesture at the party-goers. "Whoever created this lot must have had a dirty mind!"

"They're just trying to enjoy themselves. What's wrong with that?"

"How they're doing it. They should be reading elevating books, composing music or poetry, thinking high thoughts or walking in green fields and high woods. Communing with nature, not milling around gobbling smorgasbord and swilling gin."

"It's what you're doing."

"All I've had is a frilly biscuit with a very doubtful bit of anchovy on it."

"And a very large gin and tonic," said Shelagh pointedly.

"Anchovy is very salty."

"But you're here, eating and dining – you're not thinking high thoughts or wandering the fields getting intimate with nature, are you?"

"I wish I were. Unfortunately," Pat leaned over her confidentially, "my mind has been atrophied by a good education and life of luxury. Noble thoughts are beyond me. As for getting intimate with nature – there are no longer any usable lovers' lanes. They're full of abandoned cars and old fridges. But if you're interested, I've a clean and comfortable flat near Regent's Park."

"No, thank you." Shelagh edged away.

Pat followed her. "It's very quiet."

"No, thank you."

"You don't believe in sex at first sight?"

"I don't believe in answering that sort of question."

"You mean I must find out for myself?"

"I don't answer trick questions either," said Shelagh coldly. "Excuse me. I must join the other creations of a dirty mind."

She walked off into the crowded room. Pat watched her go. She was slim, elegant in a blue dress that was beautifully waisted to swing tantalisingly knee-length over perfectly formed calves above neat ankles. A fascinating sight to any discerning male.

"Interesting bottom," said Jimmy Williams. "I've always admired it."

"How is it I've not met her before?"

"She's only in town off and on, visiting Maggie. Her father's a country parson, which is why she took umbrage at your denigration of the Word."

"Parsons' daughters can be hot stuff. Lots of them become actresses." Pat sucked his lips. "What part of the country?"

"Longford Stanton, Cheltenham way. But you'd be wasting your time tripping out there. According to Maggie no man will get his hands on Shelagh Breagh's bottom until he has been duly licensed by the Lord, and Maggie is not one to lightly admit to belief in a friend's virginity."

"Virgins are only virgins because they have not been properly tempted. In the right place with the right man no woman can resist sex. It's against nature."

"And you're the right man, eh? Nature's secret weapon against virgins."

Pat shook his head. "Not in Cheltenham and district. I am an urban man. It'd take more than an attractive bottom to lure me out among the cow pats."

"Tough on you," said Jimmy Williams. "There aren't any untouched bottoms round here, attractive or otherwise."

Maggie Williams helped herself to a canapé. "He's Pat Pendle," she said in answer to Shelagh's enquiry. "What about him?"

"He invited me to his flat," said Shelagh, "within two minutes of being introduced."

"That's par for him. Give him a wide berth, duckie. He thinks women were specially created to welcome him with open thighs."

"Is he really as bad as that?"

"Worse! And there are plenty of women who agree with him. If he got married half the unwed in London would go into mourning."

Shelagh eyed Pat across the room. "He is rather good-looking."

Maggie frowned. "When are you going home?"

"Tomorrow. Why?"

"I'm not letting you out of my sight till you're on the train. And if you value that which you can't lose twice, don't come to London for at least a twelve-month. If you do you'll end up a passing ejaculation in his sperm count."

"Don't be silly. I'd never allow him to touch me."

"You think he is good-looking," Maggie said emphatically. "That is the first symptom of surrender.

He'll persuade you that you are the only woman in his life, but he won't explain that it's a limited contract with an escape clause."

Shelagh smiled disbelievingly.

"'Tis true," said Maggie. "I'm warning you. Get back on your Humps and stay there. It's your only hope. Pat Pendle is strictly a city bird. He thinks the Cromwell Road should carry a health warning."

"So it should. All those cars – lead poisoning affects the brain."

"So does Pat Pendle. Go home and stay there."

A Meeting of the Fathers

When Good King Hal decided that the monasteries of Britain had more wealth than was good for their spiritual health, and set about depriving them of their worldly goods for the benefit of their heavenly bounty and his earthly treasure, the Abbot of Longford Stanton was not pleased, and refused to cooperate. This annoyed Henry so he knocked down the Abbey and beheaded the Abbot, who is reputed to walk the ruins weeping and wailing and looking for his head, Henry having buried it separately to cause the Abbot more discomfort when the day of resurrection dawned. How one weeps and wails headless is a matter for speculation, but more than one Longford Stanton local claims to have seen and heard the apparition. However, aware that the village needed a place for worship, Henry graciously spared the chantry near the Abbey and made it the parish church, appointing the Rector himself. So Longford Stanton became a Royal Peculiar, a living in the gift of the monarch and therefore outside the jurisdiction of the bishop. It has remained so ever since. The names of the successive royal appointees from 1546 onwards are printed in gold lettering on a highly polished panel in the porch of the old chantry, now blessed by dedication to St Thomas the Doubter. The last of these names is that of the present incumbent, the Reverend Donald Breagh DD MA.

The Rectory, an over-large Victorian pile with lots of spikes and finials and bargeboards, stands at the end of a narrow lane beyond the Abbey ruins. The ruins themselves, a National Monument (open to visitors by appointment only), are approached by a lower, broader road. In consequence the lane enjoyed all the virtues of a private drive. A sign proclaimed it to be a cul-de-sac and the Rector had added another specifying *Rectory Only*. The Reverend Breagh liked his privacy.

Presently, like his unfortunate predecessor, he was not pleased.

His displeasure was directed at a large and dirty Rolls parked in the lane, completely blocking the approach to his home. The Rector pressed the horn of his own car, trying to control his annoyance. There was no response. Peering forward he saw that the car was empty. Repressing an impulse to give a louder, more demanding blast to summon the absent driver, the Rector left his car and picked his way gingerly between the hedge and ditch bordering the lane and looked inside the Rolls.

Rolls were by no means uncommon in the parish, but they were all clean and gleaming, reflecting pride of ownership. Not so this specimen! The seats were cluttered with old coats, waterproofs, and a variety of tin helmets of the kind worn by construction workers. Outside it was muddy and begrimed, two smeared arcs on the filthy windscreen illustrating the owner's apparent indifference to even the most elementary aspects of car care.

"Scandalous," muttered the Reverend Breagh, appalled at the careless treatment of so valuable an asset.

His own car was an old Morris Minor. He had chosen

it with care as peculiarly suitable to his calling, embodying quality and unpretentious humility with the virtue of a shrewd investment of increasing worth. It also, he thought, gave him an air of mild and endearing eccentricity, the embodiment of an English country parson: caring, gently humorous, learned and liberal, ever ready with a kindly hand for the needy and a word of comfort for those in pain or trouble. He cultivated the role assiduously – but as he possessed an alarmingly short-fused temper his performance was never likely to get him nominated for an Oscar.

The Rector looked around. There was no sign of the driver, but alongside the empty car an open gate gave onto an uncultivated field thick with thistles, bindweed, brambles and coarse grass. At the far end two oak trees framed a gap in the hills that kept Longford Stanton apart from Longford Proper, once a depressed mining town but now enjoying a boom as the silicon belt expanded westwards from Cirencester and more distant Swindon. A man was standing by one of the oaks, his back to the gate. At first the Rector thought he was attending to the wants of nature but, as the man turned, he realised that he was surveying the field.

A cascade of pennies rattled in the Rector's mind. Pitts was at it again! No doubt the recent crass housing policy announced by the government had encouraged him. Well! The Reverend Breagh strode purposefully into the field, each step edging his temper towards boiling point. Mr Eric Pitts was the *bête noire* of the village, and in nobody's eyes was he more *noir* than the Rector's. The battle to thwart Pitts's plan to cover the field with desirable executive dwellings was still fresh in his mind, as indeed was the knowledge that they would all have been plainly visible from the Rectory! Any attempt by Pitts to resurrect the proposal had to be nipped in the bud, quickly.

"What the devil do you think you're up to?" he

demanded.

The man who turned to meet his question wore a flat cap, torn donkey jacket, and trousers so baggy that the crotch was between his knees. A thick growth of stubble decorated his chin and shaggy eyebrows were bushed over a bent nose. An unlit, thin cigar protruded from his lips. The whole was covered with a thin layer of grey dust and appeared to have recently emerged from a bath in a chalk pit.

"Uh?" he grunted.

In a less combative mood the Reverend Breagh might have paused to wonder how such a creation could possibly be the product of a benevolent Almighty but his mind was on more material things.

"I asked you what the devil you're doing in this field."

"What am I doing here?"

"Don't repeat my question! Answer it!"

"How d'y'mean?"

The Reverend choked. "What do you mean, how do I mean? I asked what you are doing in this field and I expect an answer! I repeat, what are you doing here?"

The man plucked the cigar from his mouth as if disbudding a rose bush.

"You want to know what I'm doing here?"

"Good God man, haven't I made it plain enough? What are you doing here?"

"Is it yourn? This field?"

"That is beside the point. Kindly answer my question. What are you doing in this field?"

"It ain't yourn then?"

The Rector seethed. "Will you tell me at once what you are doing here?"

"You really want to know?"

"How many times do I have to repeat myself? It is what I have asked you twenty times. I demand an answer."

"And you're gunna get one too – it's none of your

business. You don't own it so keep your nose out."

With a flick of his thumb the man tossed his cigar butt into the air and walked past the Rector towards the gate.

The bells in the chantry beyond chimed as if heralding a wedding march.

The Virgin at Home

"Obscene?" said Mrs Breagh. "Obscene?"

"Yes, mother. Obscene."

"Then don't tell your father. You know he hates swearing."

"He didn't swear. He said the word was obscene."

"Obscene?" repeated Mrs Breagh disbelievingly. "Obscene?"

"Yes, mother. Obscene."

"An obscene word is a swear word. Surely you know that?"

"But... Oh never mind."

"I'm surprised at Maggie inviting such a person to her party. She's usually very particular."

Shelagh gave up and wandered to the window. Her mother's ability to misunderstand things was as exasperating as a *Guardian* misprint. The man Pendle had been exasperating too, but undeniably attractive and, until his direct sexual invitation disconcerted her into a defensive retreat, she had rather liked his teasing, amused attitude to life. After all, despite his disparaging remarks about religion and his sexual effrontery, he had criticised contemporary materialism and neglect of the countryside – sentiments central to her work at the Western Ecological Preservation Society. And he had a nice face, with soft grey eyes. Whatever Maggie Williams might think she felt sure he was not completely bad. Handled the right way she was sure...

Her mother's voice interrupted her reverie. "Are you sure you threw it this way?"

"What?"

"The ring. Are you sure…?"

"Of course I'm sure. How many times do you want telling!"

"Did it hit anything?"

"I've told you that too. I don't know. He dodged. If he hadn't he would have caught it."

"Really, Shelagh, you can't expect a man to stand and catch what you might throw at him even if he was expecting it and…"

"He was expecting it. I told him he could have it back and… Oh, never mind. If he wants it let him come and find it."

Shelagh turned impatiently back to the window. Her mother gave an audible "Tut" and ran her arm between the cushions of the deep, loose-covered settee. She had searched the room meticulously a score of times since Shelagh had stormed from the sitting room, announced her engagement to Andrew Hawkins was off, and gone to bed without another word.

Mrs Breagh had found Andrew scrabbling about on the floor looking for the antique diamond and sapphire engagement ring Shelagh had thrown at him when announcing that she never wanted to see his face again. Clearly the breach had been preceded by something more than a lovers' tiff. But, despite discreet questioning by both families, neither party to it was prepared to reveal the cause. All that was known was that Shelagh had thrown the ring at her ex-beloved, and it had not been seen since.

It was an embarrassing situation for the Reverend and Mrs Breagh. The Hawkins had been very understanding but the ring was valuable. They hoped it would be found. They hoped not only that it would be found but that the two young people would become reconciled and eventually married. It was a hope Mrs Breagh fervently shared, and she felt sure that finding the ring was the key needed for the opening of peace talks. Had she known her daughter's mind she would not have been so sure.

Shelagh had returned to speculating about Pat Pendle's eyes, unsure now whether what she had thought was grey might not have been a shade of blue. And she was wishing she had asked Maggie more about him – surely he did something more than chase women? What, for instance, did he do for a living? It was a pity, too, that she'd left him so abruptly when he'd mentioned sex. At least he had been straightforward and open about it. Rather different from Andrew's furtive attempt to get a hand up her skirt! Shelagh suppressed a giggle. It had not actually been his clumsy effort at seduction that had annoyed her. Men were like that and a girl had to expect it. But when she'd told him to behave he said she was like his mother. That was too much! Mrs Hawkins was fat, condescending and treated her son as if he were still a schoolboy. Not at all the vision a man should have of his future wife. The final straw in the argument had been his claim that he meant it as a compliment! If there had been something more lethal than the engagement ring handy she would have thrown that at him.

Pat Pendle's approach was much more honest, if misguided. After all, sex was a perfectly natural function, like eating and sleeping, and Shelagh approved of all things natural – except pre-marital sex. Friends frequently scoffed at her reticence, arguing that marriage was an institution devised by men to preserve their property, while sex was a perfectly natural physical need that could be freely indulged, particularly as modern science had divorced the pleasure of the act from the penalty. But to Shelagh the first act of sex, the loss of virginity, was a kind of baptism, presaging a future of love and happiness. Not necessarily in marriage but in commitment, loyalty to another in body and soul.

She considered her outlook natural. She was a nature girl, she worked with nature through the WEPS, and outdoors nature was in the full swing of spring: the sun shone brightly on a patchwork of green and brown fields and in the hedgerows birds were busy doing natural things naturally. In the distance a gleam of silver marked where the Langye curved away from Stanton Humps to meet the broader Severn beyond Stanton Proper. Flocks of seagulls pursued a tractor and plough across White's ten-acre and two men were crossing Pitts' field. They looked as if they were arguing. At least one did, for he was gesticulating furiously. Shelagh gave a gasp!

"Mummy, Daddy's in Pitts field having an argument with somebody."

"He's gone to see Canon Foulkes about the communion wine, dear."

"It looks like a gypsy."

"He says the quality has deteriorated lately."

"Mummy, will you come and look? They'll be gone in a second."

Mrs Breagh joined her daughter at the window as the two men disappeared behind the hedge bordering the lane.

"It's been upsetting his stomach."

"They've gone now."

"Who have?"

"Daddy was down there having an argument with a man. A scruffy man."

"I can't see anyone."

"I know now but…do you think I should go and see if he's all right?"

"Are you sure it was him?"

"I should know my own father, shouldn't I?"

"You should. You've got his temper to prove it. Throwing your ring at poor Andrew."

"Oh mother!"

"Men don't like that sort of thing. It makes them uncomfortable."

"I'm going to see if Daddy's all right!"

"The Hawkins are such a good family, very respectable."

Shelagh didn't listen. She went out.

In the hall, double stained-glass doors opened onto an outer porch and the front door. Red clay tiles and a sunken heavy coarse mat lay above two steps that led down to a gravelled area bordered by laurels and a yew hedge. On either side of the front door were large square bay windows, but the symmetry was spoilt by an octagonal glass tower at one corner from which a conical heading like a dunce's cap poked above the roof. Ivy covered most of the brickwork and, where it could be seen, the paintwork was dark green with white on the window sashes. The gravelled area before the house was extensive. A large two-storeyed gable-roofed garage (formerly a coach house) stood to one side. At the apex of its gable a weathervane carried a coach and horses westwards as Sam Weller and Mr Pickwick attempted to clamber in from north and south. Wrought-iron gates set in brick piers with stone copings hung permanently open at the entrance to the drive, beyond which the lane curved round to the lower end of the village.

As Shelagh stepped from the porch a large, muddy Rolls was approaching the house from the lane. It swept into the drive towards the garage, revealing her father's Morris Minor some distance behind. Confronted by the garage the Rolls stopped, reversed and shot back across the gravelled area into a laurel bush, narrowly missing the Morris, which followed it through the gates and skidded to a halt before the garage. The Rolls immediately jerked forward and Shelagh had a fleeting glimpse of its cloth-capped driver laughing as he twisted the steering wheel and accelerated away back down the lane.

Red faced and furious her father emerged from the Morris. "Did you get his number?"

"What on earth's going on, Daddy?"

"Did you get his number?"

"No, of course not. I…"

"Damn!"

The Rector stamped down to the gates and looked after the disappearing Rolls. Shelagh followed him.

"What's happened, Daddy?"

"I couldn't get it from the back. The thing was so filthy! It's disgraceful, a car like that! Shouldn't be allowed on the road."

"Did he run into you?"

"He's was up to something in Pitts' field."

The Rector turned and stumped back towards the house. Shelagh followed him.

"What sort of thing?"

"He wouldn't tell me! But Tewson will know if anyone does."

Freedom from Information

Warwick Tewson was known as "Oh Jesus" by the mandarins of the Department of Rural Affairs, over which he reigned as Minister. The sobriquet arose from his ejaculation of the blasphemy in times of panic or crisis. These were not infrequent, for Warwick possessed no political skills other than those inherent in a born opportunist. Generally he was happy to leave all decisions to his departmental heads, except those which affected friends and colleagues. These he would consider impartially and come down in their favour, on the understanding that he would receive similar consideration where his own interests were concerned.

He had no particular interest in politics but having married the daughter of an MP with a safe seat he had, on his father-in-law's death, gratefully accepted the opportunity to take his place. Warwick knew a bargain when he saw one. Salaried membership of the best club in London with only the tedium of an electoral gesture every four years or so as entrance fee.

When Rural Affairs was created to satisfy the screams of environmentalists, Warwick was deemed an ideal candidate for the post for, as the PM remarked to the Chancellor, they needed a man who could be relied on to initiate nothing and didn't know what a principle was. Warwick had recognised this as another bargain! A minister was more or less assured of a title on retirement and with it would come membership of the even more exclusive other house. What better place to idle away one's declining years – with pay!

"Oh Jesus!" said the Minister of Rural Affairs and removed his feet from his desk to study more closely the document he was reading. It was the weekly circular detailing planning and project decisions. Usually he glanced at them with no more attention than a begging letter, or a constituent's plea for some favour, before throwing them aside for the usual channels to deal with. But that mysterious force that somehow immediately focuses one's eyes on one's name on a crowded page will do the same for other items of self-interest. Warwick had immediately homed in on an item which read: *Stanton Humps: License 284967/S/QB. Waste infilling. Pendle's Disposal Confirmed.*

Oh Jesus Makes a Point

At precisely four o'clock each working day, meetings, conferences, briefs and other important circumstances permitting, Joseph Porson, Permanent Under-Secretary to the Ministry of Rural Affairs, enjoyed a cup of Keemun, the favourite tea of Boswell and Doctor Johnson. He liked to linger over the smooth, light liquor, taking slow sips, savouring the flavour, imagining himself among the brilliant conversationalists and wits of the eighteenth century. It was at such times that he concocted the elegant witticisms with which he sought to delight his fellow mandarins on the various committees that regulated the whims of their respective ministers.

The cup was halfway to his lips, the fumes pervading his nostrils, tantalising his taste buds with anticipatory delight as he considered the wisdom of telling a certain female Permanent Secretary that she should wear curtains more often, when the door of his office was flung open with such startling violence that he rose from his chair in alarm and spilt the steaming liquid delight all over his flies.

"What the bloody hell", yelled his minister, "is all this about?"

He threw a bound memorandum onto the Under-Secretary's desk.

"Yow!" yelled the wit *manqué*, clutching his bifurcation.

"Why wasn't I consulted? Why wasn't I told?"

"Oh my God!"

"Get it cancelled. Withdrawn, annulled, pigeonholed, anything! But get the damn thing stopped. Understand?"

"But Minister…"

"Never mind the bloody 'buts', get it done."

"I am scalded, Minister! I need attention. I must leave

the room."

"If I don't get word from you within fifteen minutes that that idiot licence is revoked you'll be leaving something more than this room. So get on with it!"

Oh Jesus Tewson went out with as much violence as he had entered.

The ultimatum was ticking away its last thirty seconds when Porson, his trousers replaced but his dignity still ruffled, stood before his minister to register a protest. It fell on deaf ears.

"Have you got the licence revoked?"

"There are standards, Minister," said Porson doggedly, "and it is in the interests of both of us to observe them. I..."

"Damn your interests, and in future don't keep me in ignorance of what's happening to mine in my own ministry."

"I am not aware," said Porson stiffly, "that I have kept the Minister in ignorance of anything. Quite the contrary. The boot, if I may use the metaphor, is on other foot."

"What?"

"It is I who am being kept in ignorance. And if I may say so," continued Porson, unable to resist the temptation, "*Felix qui potuit rerum cognoscere causas.*"

Oh Jesus stared uncomprehendingly. "Am I supposed to know what you're talking about?"

"I would be happier," Porson translated triumphantly, "if I knew what you were talking about."

"The waste infill at Stanton Humps. You know damn well that it's in my constituency. You should have put me in the picture before authorising this tip. Get it revoked."

"I thought the Minister's house was at Longford Stanton?"

"It is, and it overlooks the Humps. The bloody tip'll be more or less in my back garden. Get it stopped."

Joseph Porson felt the thrill of *schadenfreude*. "I'm afraid that is impossible, Minister."

"What?"

"The matter is outside our remit."

"Don't be stupid," said Tewson scornfully. "My remit is Rural Affairs and there is nowhere in the country more rural than Stanford Humps. I know – I live there, don't I?"

"That may be so, Minister, but in certain circumstances…"

"Never mind your 'maybes' and circumstances. I'm not having anything dumped on the Humps. Is that clear?"

"Your intention is clear, Minister, but it is…"

"Stop giving me 'buts'! It would ruin the view from my sitting room so tell whoever's idea it was to get stuffed."

"But Minister…"

"For Christ's sake," said Tewson, exasperated beyond measure. "Just get on with it."

Porson said, "You wish me to tell the members of the Cabinet individually, Minister?"

Tewson, about to leave the room, stopped as if suddenly meeting a brick wall. "What?"

"The minister may not have noticed", continued Porson, hardly able to suppress a smirk of satisfaction, "that it is a Cabinet decision and classified as Top Secret under the Freedom of Information Act."

"Top Secret?" said Tewson incredulously. "A bloody tip a top secret! What…what'll be in it? What'll they be tipping?"

"Obviously that is not for us to know, Minister. We are being informed simply as a matter of courtesy. No doubt because it would not do for the Minister to be kept in complete ignorance of what is to happen in his constituency."

There was no mistaking Porson's insinuation.

Either accidentally or by design the Cabinet had snubbed Tewson in a manner that required a strong protest, a threat of resignation. But he was well aware that neither would cut much ice with the PM – it might even be used to get rid of him! Warwick Tewson was not biting that!

"May I express my sympathy with the Minister's predicament," said Porson, happily reading his thoughts.

"Go to hell!"

"Certainly, Minister."

Porson departed triumphantly to a fresh cup of Keemun. Tewson sat at his desk and tried to work out how he should react to the situation. The prospect of a tip on the Humps was bad enough – a tip protected by 'Top Secret'… It had to be something too nasty to contemplate.

One thing he saw clearly and it worried him deeply. Secret or not, the infill could not be kept hidden from the locals and as soon as a start was made, or was even rumoured, property prices in Longford Stanton would nosedive – and none more steeply than that of his own house, the terrace of which looked directly over the Humps. He stood to lose thousands, even supposing he was able to sell at all once the infill was under way. It was not a pleasant prospect.

His pondering was interrupted by a call from the Rector of Longford Stanton, who wanted to know if the Minister could spare him a few moments of his valuable time.

Tewson hesitated. The Rector was his immediate neighbour and his first thought was that rumours of the infill were already abroad, and if the call was to register protest it might be best to put it off, play for time. Second thoughts reminded him that as the matter was top secret and he had nothing to fear – yet.

"Put the Rector through," he said.

The Rector wasted no time in getting to the point. Tewson listened to a recital of the events in Pitts field with some relief. There was a possibility that the rough visitor might be connected with the coming infill rather than housing on Pitts' field but, even if he was, nothing would have been said, the Freedom of Information Act took care of that. He assured the Rector that there were no plans that he knew of but he would make enquiries and report back as soon as possible. Then he pleaded urgent business, rang off and returned to the vexed problem of how to save his principal financial asset, his house.

Somehow he had to sell before the work started or any hint of it became known. How long did he have? Days? Weeks? Months? How could he find out? He could hardly ask the PM or a Cabinet member as it would... A name on the memorandum caught his eye. Pendle. It was the name of the contractor... Pendle? He knew that name. Pendle.... Pendle...? He scratched his chin, searched his memory awhile, then reached for the telephone.

Pat Pendle's phone rang as he was ruminating on Shelagh Breagh's attractive bottom, wondering whether it really was as inaccessible as everyone believed.

Tom Tries it On – A Dress

Old Tom Pendle replaced his wife's dress in the wardrobe and clambered into his flannel trousers, pulling the thick belt tightly round his waist. For all his sixty years he carried little excess fat. Washed and shaven after his trip to inspect the infill site at Longford Stanton he was scarcely recognisable as the tramp-like labourer who had clashed with the Rector. But that was old Tom's way.

"That's me working," he'd say to his sons. "Only cocks wear their best on dunghills."

Before going downstairs he took another look at the dress. It was white and red, his favourite colour combination, but a bit tight round the waist. Either Dolly was losing weight or he'd put on a bit.

The dining room was empty when he entered but he could hear Dolly in the kitchen. He sat at the table and surveyed the meal. Neatly cut sandwiches and a variety of cup cakes and vanilla slices.

"Dolly?"

"Yes, Tom."

"Where's the Swiss roll?"

"Isn't it there?"

"I can't see it."

Dolly came from the kitchen looking flushed and warm. "I thought I put a new one there."

"Jam or chocolate?"

"You had a chocolate one yesterday."

"I know. That's why I want to make sure I get a jam one today. I like 'em changed and changed about."

"I know that, Tom."

"So I'll have a jam one today."

"I thought I'd put one there."

"Well, you haven't."

"I'm sorry, Tommy."

"Never mind, just get one."

Dolly went into the kitchen and returned a moment later with a pot of tea and a Swiss roll still in its carton. She put down the pot, pushed a wisp of grey hair from her head and began to remove the wrapping from the Swiss roll.

"I'll do that. You pour the tea."

"Yes, Tommy."

She handed him the carton and busied herself arranging the cups and saucers. Tom Pendle unwrapped the roll and placed it on the cake stand between the cup cakes and vanilla slices.

"I feel like a bit of Swiss roll," he said.

"I got the vanilla slices from Yorick's. They looked so nice and fresh."

"Right. I'm looking forward to one of them too."

"I thought you would."

Dolly poured thick, dark tea into one of the cups and passed it to Tommy, who added milk and two heaped spoons of sugar. He liked it strong and sweet. She preferred hers somewhat weaker, so the second cup was only half filled and water added.

The room in which the Pendles were starting their tea was large and perfectly square. The table, as square as the room, stood in the centre between a sepia-tiled fireplace, stepped like a corbie gable, and an enormous sideboard loaded with decorative chinaware. A pair of brass candlesticks placed incongruously on the outer corners of the top shelf had long red candles wedged in their sconces. A chandelier with imitation flame bulbs and thin glass pendants hung above the table, around which were four straight-backed dining chairs with highly polished rexine seats. There were more candlesticks on the lowest of the fireplace's corbie steps, but these were porcelain miniatures with square bases and a motif of tiny red roses on the stems. The other steps supported framed photographs, and the top bore a bulbous vase with artificial roses. Dead centre on each of the four walls hung a framed picture of animals. A dog begging, horses running by the sea, robins in snow and, in pride of place over the hearth, a group of kittens lapping cream. A sash window with floral curtains looked out on a yard where the back of a parked lorry completely obscured whatever was beyond.

"Yorick's had doughnuts too," said Dolly, "but they were 50p. That's a lot for a doughnut."

"How much were these?" Tom dug into a vanilla slice.

"Vanilla slices aren't easy like doughnuts. You have to layer vanilla slices with puff pastry and they've cream in as well as jam – doughnuts only have jam. Doughnuts are easy."

"So how much were they?"

"I bought them as a special treat, Tom, so I'm not telling."

"You don't have to feel guilty. I've told you, spend what you like. We've plenty."

"But you never know, do you? There's rainy days that come when you don't expect them, and milk's gone up again, did I tell you?"

Tom Pendle sighed. Throughout the length and breadth of Britain Pendle's lorries, vans, tankers and trains moved domestic rubbish and the waste products of industry hither and thither, processing it, burning it, burying it, importing and exporting it, depositing it in old quarries, pits, mines or any other convenient hole in the ground, anywhere and everywhere. There was nothing too filthy, too foul, stinking, dirty, gross, putrid or dangerous for Pendle's to successfully dispose of – at a price.

Shifting the shit of Britain had made Tom a multi-millionaire but his wife still counted the pennies as she had done when he had been a humble totter scavenging the tips for saleable wares.

"Dolly," he said patiently. "If it rained cats and dogs for the next month you could still afford to buy anything you wanted."

"Oh yes," said Dolly sceptically.

"Money doesn't matter any more."

"Why did you ask how much the vanilla slices were then?"

"I was just interested, with you going on about the price of doughnuts."

"I wasn't going on, I was remarking. Fifty pence is ten shillings as was. Ten shillings for a doughnut! It's scandalous really."

"We can afford it."

"Maybe now, yes, but there's always tomorrow, don't

forget that!"

Tom finished his vanilla slice and reached for the Swiss roll. He had fought the battle with Dolly for too long to expect to convince her and, in his heart, he was proud that his wife was as unaffected by their wealth as he was. They still lived as they had always lived, only more so.

"Besides," said Dolly, "we have to think of the children. I don't want to die without leaving them a bit of money to help them on their way."

"They'll be all right. I've seen to that. They'll get the business."

"Businesses can go wrong."

"Ours won't – there's more muck now in the world than there's ever been."

"So you say, but all the same I've a bit put by from the housekeeping so they'll get that from me. That's safe, whatever happens. Are you having a second slice?"

Tom shook his head. "I'll finish with one of them cup cakes."

"I'll put it back in the wrapping then," said Dolly practically. "Save it going stale."

CHAPTER TWO

Honesty's the Best Hypocrisy

Pat Pendle was idly stirring a Martini in Crindles of Brook Street and thinking of Shelagh Breagh. It was not often that Pat allowed his mind to dwell on any particular female. Women came into his life as easily as the daily press – examined, digested and cast aside without further thought. Not that he was an unthinking man; Pat thought a great deal about life and what it was and might or might not be. His conclusion was that it was really some kind of cosmic con-trick. Man had been sold shares in an enterprise on the basis of a shiny mellifluous prospectus full of promises of earthly joy and happiness that had no reality. Who had prepared the prospectus was a matter of dispute, on which too much time was wasted in arguments that had even less reality than the prospectus. No amount of introspection, self-chastisement or good deeds was going to alter the fact that Man was up the creek without a paddle.

The only thing to do was to stop bothering about the boat and find what solace was available in the creek. Aided by his father's fortune and indulgence, Pat devoted his time to doing just that. He frequented the best clubs and restaurants and enjoyed the best available women. It was the unavailability of Shelagh Breagh that was occupying his thoughts when Warwick Tewson approached him.

"Nice of you to come at such short notice, old man,"

said Warwick.

They shook hands, Pat wincing slightly at the familiarity. Beyond being aware that the family's waste disposal company had frequent dealings with the Ministry of Rural Affairs, he knew Warwick only from occasional meetings at the cycle of parties, charity events and other organised activities that went to make up the capital's social year. The call suggesting a meeting had been a surprise, particularly the request for 'a private chat' on a matter that could not be mentioned on the telephone.

A waiter came and Warwick ordered a whisky. Pat refused another Martini. They exchanged a few pleasantries.

"You were at the Williams's do, I hear."

"Was there anyone who wasn't?"

"Margaret always invites too many people; there's never room to move."

"You didn't ask me to come here to talk about the Williamses, did you?"

"No, no! What I wanted to chat about was this infill at Stanton Humps."

"The what?"

"There's a bit of a problem there and I need your cooperation to get it sorted out. Nothing terribly difficult, just a matter of adjusting the starting date. You don't have a contractual starting date, do you?"

"I don't know what you're talking about."

"The infill at Stanton Humps, old chum. Your firm has the licence for it – or perhaps you don't know that yet, probably hasn't reached your office. In fact there might well be a bit of a delay." Warwick lowered his voice slightly. "It's an Official Secret, so forms will have to be signed. But you can take my word, old man, the contract is yours."

Pat stared at the Minister. Although a director, for tax and hierarchical reasons, he took no part in the activities of

Pendle's Disposal. It was on the tip of his tongue to explain this but the mention of 'Official Secret' aroused his curiosity. It explained the reticence over the telephone and the request for privacy. It also sounded pretty incredible.

"There's going to be an infill, and it's an Official Secret?"

Warwick nodded.

"You're joking surely."

"Never more serious in my life, old chum. There are various reasons for the decision, which naturally I can't reveal."

"But it's absurd! How can you keep an infill a secret? You can't make people pass it with their eyes shut!"

"The local people will know, of course, but there'll be no publicity. The media will be kept off. Not allowed to mention it."

"Can you do that?"

"With the revised Freedom of Information Act, old man, we can do anything! Commercial confidentiality. National security."

"National security on a tip?"

Warwick lifted a hand and broadened his lips to a smile which was intended to convey a shared incredulity at the ways of governments, and his inability to reveal anything.

"I've never heard anything so barmy in all my life!" said Pat. "What about the drivers? They'll know."

"They'll have to sign, pledge to say nothing. So will the old guffer I think your lot may have sent down to look over the site." Warwick sipped his whisky. "I had a call from the Rector, who saw him snooping around Pitts field and thinks it's someone having another shot at building houses there. He's bound to get the truth in time, of course, but it wouldn't do for it to leak out before the actual infilling starts. Among other things it'd ruin any chance I have of selling my house before the bottom drops out of the housing market there, and that's why I want a bit of cooperation from you – I need at least eight clear weeks before you make a start. Can you manage that?"

There was a complete confidence in Warwick's tone, as if the request between old chums was so reasonable that it couldn't possibly be refused.

Pat was intrigued. He knew at once that the 'old guffer' was his father, who always took a great interest in any major site the company acquired. Despite his massive wealth and the fact that Pendle's Disposal was a plc, Tom Pendle remained very much a practical hands-on man: others, directors, did the paper work, kept the office running smoothly. He kept the power. As usual, he'd been down to Stanford Humps to 'weigh up the how d'you dos' as he'd put it.

Plainly Warwick Tewson was seeking his help in looking after Number One, confirming Pat's belief that all politicians were self-interested creeps. But something else was ringing a bell in the verges of his memory and he couldn't quite place it or bring it clearly to mind.

"Where did you say this place is?" he asked.

"Stanton Humps. D'you know it?"

"I thought you said Pitts."

"That's the field. It could be used for lorries to get to the Humps, which is what your man was about, I suppose. My house overlooks part of it, so does the Rectory. They've been trying to build houses on it but I soon put a stop to that – with Breagh's help, of course, but this waste business is…"

"Longford Stanton! The Rector of Longford Stanton!"

"What?"

"I didn't connect the Stanton Humps with Longford Stanton, but I remember now. Not far from Stoke Kirby! A range of hills?"

"That's right. The Pomfreys live there. Stoke Kirby. Do you know them?"

"Yes, I do, as a matter of fact. But…"

"The infill won't affect them. Stoke Kirby's the other side of Longford, but the damn thing'll ruin the view from my terrace."

Pat's mind had jumped to other things. The attractive, untouchable bottom! "The Rector's daughter is called Shelagh? Right?"

"Yes, nice girl. You've met her?"

"Yes, at the Williams's."

"They're my neighbours."

"Really."

"The infill will ruin their view too, but there's nothing they can do about that. Tied cottage, a Rectory – goes with the job. Different with me. I could be thousands out of pocket. Who's going to buy a house with a tip in front of it?"

"Nobody with any sense, I imagine."

"Exactly. Which is why I want you to hold off the start until I've sold it."

"What about searches? Planning permission?"

"Not needed. The Humps are government land, and it's a Cabinet decision. Good grief! Can you imagine the uproar there'd be if they had to get a local decision? That's why it's been kept quiet – they never even let on to me, the bastards!"

This last point rankled Warwick deeply. It was something he intended to turn his attention to when the sale of his house had been accomplished. Some so-called friends were in for a verbal onslaught. Do-as-you-would-be-done-by hadn't been done.

"Aren't you supposed to reveal to the buyer anything that might affect the value of the property you're selling?"

"Can't do that, old man," Warwick grinned.

"Wouldn't do for a Minister of the Crown to breach the Freedom of Information Act, would it?"

Pat hesitated. Warwick took it for granted that they were of like mind when it came to self-interest and, despite the feeling that somehow the situation could possibly be exploited to renew his acquaintance with Shelagh Breagh, Pat felt it necessary to disabuse him. Warwick, however, mistook his hesitation for a bargaining ploy. He imagined Pat was waiting for the sweetener.

"We've a big gravel-moving job coming up in Dorset shortly and I'd like you to be on the selective tendering list for that. I'll probably make the choice in about eight weeks." He paused and added meaningfully, "If I've nothing else on my mind, that is."

Pat decided to administer the disabusement.

"Don't you think you're being a bit of a shit?"

But Warwick was completely unmoved.

"Of course I'm a shit. I'm a politician. Do you expect me to be a saint?"

Pat laughed, completely disarmed by the frankness.

Warwick snorted. "It's not funny! It's tragic. Self-interest is a common human failing the English refuse to make allowances for. It's why they get such rotten politicians. We have to pretend that everything we do is in the public interest – ergo we become practising hypocrites – shits."

"You're hardly being hypocritical with me."

"Sometimes honesty's the best hypocrisy – if I thought lying would win with you I'd be in there lying. But it wouldn't work, would it? You're in the shit business too...and if you're after Shelagh Breagh you're wasting your time – she's famous among Stanford males for guarding her virginity like Sir Galahad guarded his honour."

"What makes you think she interests me?"

"Instinct, old chum; the light in your eye when her name came up, and it's well known that you're handy between other men's sheets."

"Quite wrong. I abhor adultery. I attach myself only to the unattached."

"She's that all right – was engaged to the Hawkins's boy, Andrew, but she broke it off – nobody knows why. Bit of a mystery locally, cos he's as batty as she is over getting back to nature."

"She's into conservation, is she?"

Warwick nodded. "Works for some environmental outfit dedicated to the *status quo* ante. You'll probably find her lying down inviting the lorries to drive over her rather than the local flora and fauna. She's crazy about rare species – get her on the red-speckled newt and she's at your feet – unfortunately it's no help in getting her into bed."

"You've tried?"

"I'm a man, old chum. Married, but I still like my wild oats – who doesn't? And all I've got from Shelagh Breagh is a slap on the porringer, telling me not to call again."

Pat sensed again the challenge he had experienced at the Williams's. There had been too many easy conquests. A seduction requiring subtlety and careful approach work was appealing – especially when a trim figure and flashing eyes promised a victory that would be well worth the trouble of an arduous campaign.

Warwick broke into his dreaming. "Can I rely on you then? Keep off the site till I've sold my house."

Pat mused a moment on how far a girl might go in the hope of saving the flora and fauna of the Stanford Humps and said he couldn't promise anything but it might help if he took a look at the site.

"Be my guest," said Warwick. "I'm going down tomorrow, come with me."

"It might be an idea," said Pat.

"I'll get my wife to ask Shelagh to dinner," said Warwick baiting the hook. "They're great pals and you'll get an eyeful if nothing else."

Pat never resisted temptation. He took the hook and intended to take the bait.

Warwick proclaimed their amity worthy of another drink and called the waiter.

Oh Jesus in Bed

Sylvia Tewson was not surprised when her husband told her over the telephone that he was bringing a guest for the weekend. Although she took no active part in her husband's political life she was quite accustomed to entertaining politicians. It was not a task she enjoyed but she was a practical woman and knew that it was an essential part of his job.

"And ask Shelagh Breagh to dinner," he said. "Pendle's keen on her…"

"On Shelagh?"

"He met her at the Williams's and he's pally with the Pomfreys too, but I can't say more now. I'll ring tomorrow and let you know what time to expect us."

"But if he's keen on…"

"Bye."

Warwick rang off.

Sylvia put down the phone, annoyed at his brisk dismissal of her desire to know more of the visitor's interest in Shelagh. It was typical of his treatment of her.

On the terrace, which commanded a breathtaking view of the Humps with the blue line of the Welsh Hills beyond, she sat down and tried to get her life into perspective. She had no illusions about Warwick. He was money-grabbing, opportunistic and unfaithful, his only redeeming feature a total lack of shame. A kind of honesty, she presumed – if honesty could exist without any perception of morality. She had no illusions, either, about why she had married him. For a brief period she had believed that he loved her, but that had been more self-deception than illusion. She had wanted to believe that he loved her; for that matter, she had wanted to believe that she loved him, but the hard facts were that each had made a convenience of the other. He wanted the safe seat that had been more or less her family's perk for generations.

And she – well, nature had not dealt her a good hand in the sexual selection stakes. Plain, dumpy with no compensating vivacity to overcome her lack of physical appeal, there had been no suitors before Warwick. He had seen her as an investment; at twenty-nine she had seen him as an escape from looming spinsterhood. And bodily contact with a man, the relief of pent-up sexual desire, however clumsily achieved, had made her a better and happier woman. Before long, however, she came to realise that Warwick as a lover was, as in everything else, a complete bore. Unimaginative, possessing neither technique nor finesse. Roll over, bang! and "How was that, old girl?" summed up his capacity as a lover...and he expected her to lie down for him at any hour of the day or night, with "What about a couple of minutes of fun, eh?" his only enticement to intercourse. After eight years of marriage she knew who had got the better bargain!

Of her own sexuality she was now uncertain. She knew it was unsatisfied; what took place on the matrimonial bed ought to be more exciting and enjoyable than it was. But it was not that alone.

Behind the trees to one side of Pitts field Sylvia could see the conical belvedere of the Rectory. Warwick's request to invite Shelagh to dinner for the benefit of the guest who was 'keen on her' disturbed her in a way she found difficult to define, reminding her of the relief she had felt when Shelagh's engagement to Andrew Hawkins had come to naught.

Empire of Shit

Old Tom Pendle was admiring himself in Dolly's long wardrobe mirror when Dolly called from below.

"Pat's here."

"Oh – tell him I'll be down in a minute."

With some reluctance Tom uncrossed his legs and stood up, smoothing the soft satin dress over his knees and turning slightly to one side to admire the way it clung to his buttocks as the hem swirled from the movement of his hips. He'd had a hard job persuading Dolly to buy it, for red was not her favourite colour.

"It doesn't suit me."

"Course it would. What's wrong with it?"

"I'd look a scarlet woman in it."

"Gerron!" He'd thrust a wad of notes into her hand. "Go on in and buy it."

"It's an extravagance."

"I'm paying, so I'm the judge of that."

So she'd gone in. He'd stood looking in at the window while the assistant removed it from the model. Fortunately Dolly was not a small woman and he, though sturdy and tough, was not a big man so it was possible to indulge in what she called his 'funny little ways' without difficulty. In fact it rather pleased her, for her favourite occupation was window-shopping and, unlike most husbands, Tom was always willing to accompany her. Together they would spend happy hours admiring and discussing the displays in dress shops, shoe shops and anywhere where female garments and accessories were on show. Dolly was conservative in her choice of clothes and underwear. Tom frequently urged her to be more adventurous, with little success, for she was stubborn in her own way.

"It's all very well for you," she'd say. "You only try them on in the house. I have to walk out in them."

It was an argument he could not defeat. The red dress had been a small victory – indeed Dolly had never worn it, though she admitted that he looked quite smart in it.

Tom hung the dress carefully on a hanger next to an emerald green tulle dance gown, one of his favourites, and pulled on trousers and shirt. Then he carefully flushed the loo and waited for a moment before descending the stairs. Dolly would, as usual when a caller disturbed his evening fancy, have told Pat that he was 'doing a bit of business' – her euphemism for all matters pertaining to the bathroom.

Pat was smoking a cigar when Tom entered the front room. Dolly had gone into the kitchen to make a cup of tea, her immediate reaction to any visitor, family or not.

"Well, lad?"

"Fine, Dad, and you?"

"Mustn't grumble."

"Like one of these?"

Pat held out a leather cigar case but Tom declined and helped himself to a thin panatella from a cardboard packet. He liked his children to have the best but his own tastes remained what they had always been, basic working class. He judged artefacts generally by their price, with little regard to their quality. If it was expensive it was good, but this did not apply to common appetites of the body. Hence he owned a Rolls but never bought caviar, a piece of huss was better, and a cheap cigar more enjoyable than a Romeo y Juliet.

"Seen anything of Tim and Bridget?"

"They were at a party I went to a couple of days back."

"Enjoying themselves, eh?"

"It seemed like it."

"That's the way! Enjoy yourselves – all this talk of

working and slaving and having a career's a load of crap – when you've got the ready, that is. If you ain't, you've no choice. You've got to work then, but working when there's no need...barmy!"

"You still work a bit."

"Who says?"

"You're always off looking at sites – you even sometimes take a truckload out and dump it."

"That's not work! That's pleasure! Doing a dump in my own time in my own way is a pleasure to me cos it's my own choice, there's no one can push me! As for looking on sites, that's takin' a gander at me empire – an empire of shit all right, but an empire's an empire and being a boss of anything's a great feeling."

"What about this infill at Stanton Humps?"

Tom sucked his thin cigar and eyed Pat for a moment. "What's this? Never know you want to know about anything of tipping before."

"I'm going down to stay at a house nearby."

"That don't explain how you know about the tippin'."

Dolly came in with the tea. When serving it in the front room she always used the rose-patterned cups and saucers with golden rims and the reproduction Georgian silver service that was her pride and joy. When using it for the very first time she had remarked gleefully to Tom that she felt a 'real lady'. It was a feeling that had never deserted her. She put the tray down carefully on a pie-crust side table, sat equally carefully on a gold-coloured armchair with a buttoned back and lifted the pot, creating an exact replica of the advertisement that had tempted her to buy.

While Dolly was arranging herself Pat explained that his friend was in the government and had heard rumours.

"Oh yes? Well keep your trap shut about it. The shit that's going in there's nuclear coming back from abroad and we had to sign some Freedom of Information form making it an Official Secret."

Pat whistled. "The Belafield stuff the Japs don't like?"

His father nodded. "It's being shipped in at the Pollocks."

"Tom!" said Dolly.

"What?"

"We're in the front room."

Puzzle Under the Covers

When Pat had gone and they were in bed Dolly said, "Pat'll be thirty-five soon."

Tom grunted. He was thinking that what the red dress needed was a nice handbag to go with it.

"Bridget and Tim are thirty-two."

"Huh."

"I can't understand why none of them seem to think of getting married."

"Give 'em time."

"Pat's never brought the same girl here twice, and as for the twins," Dolly exhaled in puzzled exasperation, "they don't seem to have any friends at all."

"Give over, they've plenty."

"Bridget only brings girls here and Tim boys."

"Hurm."

"I thought Pat was serious with that Paula but nothing happened."

Tom grunted again. Real silk stocking with it might be an idea, if they still made 'em. He wasn't sure.

Dolly brooded quietly. Her three children moved in circles unknown to her. Each had a flat in the more select part of the West End which she rarely visited, considering them not only extravagantly expensive but unnecessary as there was ample accommodation for them in the family home. She had lived with her parents until the day she was married, and it had never entered her head to do anything else. To live alone in a flat with no one to talk to, or share meals, was to invite pity. It was something that happened to old people or others in unfortunate circumstances. She said so to Tom.

"You don't understand kids today," he said. "They see things different to how we did."

"They still get married, don't they? Have families."

"There's a lot don't see them two things going together, nowadays."

"I don't hold with that."

"Nor me neither, but it's how things are – if they don't want to marry there's no one can make 'em."

"I'm not saying anyone should, but…"

Dolly hesitated. There were deeper, more troubling matters on her mind and it needed more courage than she could muster to bring them out into the open. Her voice, when she finally spoke, was half defiant, as if challenging Tom to deny her right to raise the subject.

"What about these diseases?"

"What diseases?"

"You know. Diseases like they're getting on the telly. Where they tell you to use things to stop getting it."

"Oh," said Tom. "That!"

He had never had a serious discussion about sex in his life. He felt no embarrassment when the subject arose among his peers, and exchanged jokes and innuendoes with the best of them. With women it was different. In their company he was usually careful of speech and subdued in manner. His courtship of Dolly had been conducted at arm's length and their engagement came about more by unspoken agreement than formal proposal, Dolly's mother clinching the deal by asking Tom when he was going to name the day. Unable to counter the question as jokingly as it had been put he had mumbled that it was up to Dolly. Three months later they were in Southend-on-Sea staring at the ceiling in a darkened room until propinquity overcame their shyness and nature took its course – and so it had remained ever since. Even his dressing up in Dolly's clothes was never openly discussed. Both considered it a mild eccentricity and never gave a thought to sexual connotations as it never in any way affected their sexual behaviour. Tom, therefore, felt vaguely that Dolly's challenge to talk of sex in relation to their children was a breach of etiquette. Even when confronted by the warning AIDS advertisements on the telly they had studiously avoided mentioning them.

"We don't want them catching anything, do we?" said Dolly, easier now she had finally broken the taboo. "They'd be safer married."

Tom shifted awkwardly but said nothing. The subject irritated him.

"Don't you think they would?"

"Them things only happen to them as aren't normal. There's nothing like that about our kids."

"Oh yes, that's right," said Dolly, reassured somewhat. "But all the same, I'd be happier if they'd get married. That'd be really normal. Like us."

CHAPTER THREE

Oh Jesus Takes a Walk

Halfway to Longford Stanton the conversation turned to the Pomfreys. Warwick was of the opinion that Sir Archibald Pomfrey had been instrumental in getting the Reverend Breagh the living at the Royal Peculiar.

"He has connections with the palace. Hereditary something or other to the Royal Bedchamber and he's allowed to carry something when there's a coronation."

"Probably the Royal Pot," said Pat. "Not my joke, Paula's. It is a bowl of some sort but nobody quite knows for sure what its original use was."

"Of course, you know Paula."

"I was engaged to her once, as a matter of fact."

"You were engaged to Paula Pomfrey?"

Pat nodded, signalled, accelerated and shot past a lorry loaded with hay.

"I don't remember any announcement," said Warwick.

"There wasn't one. It was a mental aberration on my part but fortunately less than an hour after the event I introduced her to my sister, who gave her the eye and before you could say Gina Lollobrigida the engagement was off."

"Cos she didn't like your sister?"

"Oh no, quite the contrary. They liked each other very much – and Bridget has a way with her."

"Sorry, old chum, I don't get it. What happened?"

Pat laughed. "Not very easy with sex, are you?

"Sex?"

Pat nodded, keeping his eye on the road ahead.

"What do you mean? Not easy? Sex doesn't bother me – I don't get conscience-stricken over a bang-bang. I mean, it's like this, old chum. Sylvia's very accommodating but I never feel her heart's in it. I don't know if she's thinking of England when we're at it but one thing's for sure, she's not doing it cos she likes it, and naturally it affects a man's performance – takes away the enjoyment. But I feel I have to do it or she'll think I don't want her."

"I see."

"I say to her, 'How was that, old gel?' an' all I get from her is 'All right.'"

"Perhaps you should try a few variations."

"Don't be daft. She's my wife. If I started any funny stuff she'd think I was a pervert or something, and there's nothing like that about me. I'm dead normal. I take my sex straight, full frontal, on top as it's meant to be."

"There's no such thing as 'meant to be' normality, it's just a phase in evolution. For all we know our descendants may do it by remote control swinging from chandeliers – buggery may be the order of the day because ordinary procreation is no longer necessary. Babies'll be grown under glass like early tomatoes."

Outside the hedges whipped by, a blur of green. Warwick studied his companion's profile but there was no sign that Pat was being other than serious.

"I don't see what that's got to do with your sister and Paula Pomfrey."

"Bridget is a lesbian."

Warwick gave a chortle of disbelief. "And I suppose you're as gay as a buttercup."

"I'm not, actually, but Tim, my brother, Bridget's

twin, he's gay. I don't know if they got mixed up in the womb or what, but that's how it is. We must be a unique family sexually. I am a liberated hetero with a lesbian sister and a gay brother. Pretty comprehensive, don't you think? Interesting for a psychiatrist. Or do I mean psychologist? I'm always getting them mixed."

"I suppose your grandparents were transvestites!" said Warwick, with what he believed was sarcastic disbelief.

"Unfortunately they're both dead so there's no way of finding out, but my father has a tendency that way. It's amazing what there's about, you know."

"Only if you believe it!"

"It's perfectly true."

"Good Lord, look, old chum. You're playing this very poker-faced but give it a rest, eh? Let's be serious."

"I am serious."

Warwick tightened his lip. A joke was a joke but there was a time to finish it.

"You really mean you were engaged to Paula Pomfrey?"

Pat nodded. "For about twelve hours. I never gave her a ring."

"She bounced you to...to..."

"To shack up with my sister Bridget. Yes."

"But that...that...it's unbelievable."

"Why?"

"I know Paula."

"Intimately?"

"Good Lord, no, but...I don't believe this. You're pulling my leg. Must be."

Pat shrugged. They drove on in silence for a while, Warwick unable to rid himself of the suspicion that he was being teased and wondering how Sylvia would react when told that Paula was a lesbian.

"What do you know about the Pollocks?" Pat asked,

suddenly.

"Little port place, isn't it? West Coast somewhere." Pat nodded. "What about it?"

"Isn't it used for shipping nuclear stuff abroad?"

"I think so."

"All the stuff nobody wants now will be coming back there."

"Well, it's got to come in somewhere I suppose but frankly I don't give a damn..." Warwick stopped, the implication of Pat's questioning registering.

"Jesus!" he croaked. "That's not what they're going to dump on the Humps, is it?"

"According to my old man it is. They've found some deep, previously unknown, hole and it's all going in there. Then it'll be covered – the whole area of the Humps, that is – with ordinary industrial waste, so no one will ever know what is underneath." Pat glanced at his companion and smiled cynically. "No wonder it's being kept secret. If your neighbours knew what you were up to they'd probably lynch you."

Pat turned off the road into the forecourt of a half-timbered Elizabethan-looking pub beside a humpbacked bridge. Green lawns dotted with white tables and chairs ran down to a broad stream thick with rushes. It was warm with late spring sunshine so they ordered beer and sandwiches and sat under a cloudless blue sky. The only sounds were the occasional chirping of birds and a faint murmur from the stream as it trickled over a small weir.

"Like this in Longford Stanton, is it?" said Pat.

"What?"

Warwick was still digesting Pat's news about the Pollocks. He did not know exactly what was wrong with the nuclear products that were being returned: it was enough to know they were going to be dumped in Longford Humps. If he did not sell his house before a hint of what was planned leaked out then he never would.

"I asked if this was like Longford Stanton," said Pat.

"It is peaceful like this, yes. Look, are you absolutely sure it's the nuclear stuff that's going to be dumped?"

"Does it matter? You'll be safely away before anyone's poisoned – or do you mean to share your panic with your friends?"

"If I told one person, everybody'd know. It's how villages are. Change your shirt and it's public knowledge before the day's out."

"Bridget'll like that. She loves gossip."

"Who's Bridget? Oh, your sister, yes. Sorry. She's well, er...friendly with Paula Pomfrey."

"A bit more than friendly. They're shacking up together at Stoke Kirby."

"You mean she's there now?"

"More or less permanently. I believe they've plighted their feminine troths to eschew men for life."

"But..." Warwick quaked with sudden alarm. Stoke Kirby, where Paula Pomfrey was 'shacking up' with Pat's sister was part of Longford Stanton, the Reverend Breagh's parish. The Pomfrey's were churchgoers so Shelagh would certainly meet Bridget – and women gossiped. "Jesus!" Warwick broke into a cold sweat. Shelagh would tell Paula about Pat's visit, Paula would tell Sir Archibald, and before long it would be public knowledge that a director of the company carrying out the infill had been his guest just before his house was offered for sale.

Warwick shuddered as the full horror of the scenario unfolded in his mind. The infill was an Official Secret, safe from the inquisitiveness of the media, but the sale of his house wasn't. Two and two would be put together – pressmen were like that, the bastards – questions would be asked! Even more terrifying was the thought of it reaching the ears of Sykes; the Opposition's moral terrorist would be after him like a terrier after a rabbit. There'd be questions in the House.

'Would the Minister give the House his opinion of the sudden fall in house values in his constituency?'

'Does the Minister think a buyer should be compensated if a seller withholds information likely to affect the value of a property?'

'Would the Minister give details of any contracts or licences existing or being negotiated between Pendle's Disposal and his department, and is the Minister personally acquainted with any of the directors?'

It would go on and on. There would be no peace. No possibility of escape however much he stonewalled – and it would be suicidal to make an outright denial, for nosy-parkering journalists were certain to smell a juicy scandal and descend on Longford Stanton to do their investigative worst! There would be no direct mention of the infill at the Humps, oh no! The bastards were too fly for that, but there'd be all sorts of innuendoes and hints designed to get right up the PM's nostrils; and Warwick would cop it for providing the press and Opposition with a golden opportunity to harry the government over dumping in the Humps, without in any way breaking the secrecy imposed by the Freedom of Information Act.

"Bloody hell!" exclaimed Warwick. "Oh Jesus!"

"Pardon!" said Pat.

Warwick gazed dumbly at his companion. The dumbness had nothing to do with fear or embarrassment, it was simply that his normally robust instinct of self-preservation had stalled. The friendly knight promising salvation had been transformed into a threatening dragon. He needed Pat's cooperation to delay the start of the infill but having him as a house guest was definitely not on. And the problem now was how to get rid of him without offending him and losing his cooperation. For a moment or two Warwick toyed with the idea of a sudden outbreak of flu or the death of some close relative. He dismissed these, however. Flu of any virility did not happen overnight, and both he and Sylvia were curiously devoid of close family relatives.

These could be made up, of course, but that sort of lying required an underlying emotional sincerity that Warwick was incapable of simulating and, anyway, he was pretty sure Pat wouldn't be taken in.

"You look as if you've walked into a door," said Pat.

"I have in a way," said Warwick, making a lightning decision to take the bull by the horns. Honesty was the best hypocrisy! Especially when there was really no alternative. "Sylvia asked Shelagh Breagh to dinner and her first question was to ask what you did for a living!"

"So?"

"It's not going to look good later when your firm starts doing the infill."

"No problem, I can bill myself as something in the City. A Lloyd's man. That's vague enough to be anything."

"Not for Shelagh! Her father lost his lot in the City. Put it in some phoney outfit and got caught. They're still fighting to get a bit back. Say you're from the City and she'll tear you apart."

"Are you trying to frighten me off her?"

"My dear old chum, I wish you the best of luck, any man trying to lay Shelagh Breagh needs it – but there are other problems. Suppose your sister was seen in the village with Paula Pomfrey."

"Hand in hand, you mean?"

"No, seriously, listen old chum. If we're..."

Pat interrupted him irritably. "Old chums disappeared with the Empire. Why do you keep calling me one?"

"I call all my friends old chums. I..."

"Warwick," said Pat. He got up and they started to walk towards the car. "We're not friends. We're two men using each other for our own ends. To put it vulgarly, you want to save your lolly, I want to lay a Dolly."

"I say! That rhymes!"

"So it'd be better for both of us if you cut out the 'old chums', stopped shilly-shallying, and told me why you are looking as if your face had lost an argument with a barn door!"

"Can't help shilly-shallying a bit," said Warwick with the shamelessness that was his greatest charm, especially when cornered. "Being a politician I naturally tend to try and hide what I'm up to – honesty's a sort of last resort. The fact is I'm only safe if I'm absolutely in the clear over this infill business vis-à-vis selling my house. If it gets about that I've had a director of the firm doing the infilling as a guest – well! Obvious, isn't it? I'll be an Aunt Sally. In short, old chu...in short I made a boner inviting you to stay for the weekend. Your sister's hanging round the village, you could run into each other, and even if you don't, Shelagh knows your name. Think of it, Pendle – Pendle's Disposal will be all over the trucks dumping on the Humps. There's no escape, old chu...the situation is fraught."

"So?"

"Well...embarrassing this. I mean, look. I have to cover my tracks... If I have you in my house it'll be like opening a motorway. See what I mean – apart from anything else, villages are full of bloody gossips and... Well, I should have thought of it before. Can't think why I didn't – so could you sort of forget I asked you?"

"You'd like me to go back to London?"

"Only way, isn't it? Hard luck, apologies for putting you out and all that but the fact is I can't afford to be squeamish about this – I'm not a rich man, most of my money is in that house..."

"So I imagine is that of a lot of other people's round the Humps."

"There's no way that can be helped...and you've got to look after Number One in this world. No good being self-sacrificing just to be virtuous – and naturally as soon as the dust's died down you'll be a welcome guest. That's really honest – it's been a pleasure knowing you."

Pat hesitated. Torn between admiration for Warwick's blatant self-interest and annoyance at losing the chance to meet up with Shelagh Breagh again, he was tempted to embarrass Warwick by insisting on the invitation being honoured.

Instead he waited till they reached the car then asked Warwick what he'd tell his wife.

"Oh she'll understand, no bother there."

"And Shelagh?"

"You've caught a cold – terrible. Doctor prescribed no travelling, warm bed, whisky and no visitors," said Warwick. "And frankly," he added as Pat remained silent, "to put it on the line, if you've got your eye on Shelagh Breagh, forget it. You'd have more chance of a jump in a nunnery."

"You think so?"

"I know so, and every man in Stanford would tell you the same."

"Right," said Pat. "I'll get back to London."

"I'll not forget this, old chum."

Warwick took Pat's hand and shook it vigorously and they parted but as Pat turned the starter he came running back.

"I'll need a lift – this place is the middle of nowhere!"

Pat pointed to a sign across the way from the Inn. It informed the reader that Wether Blewitt station was only a mile up the lane.

"As Minister of Rural Affairs I think you should take a look at your responsibilities. And I'm sure the walk will do you good as well."

"Walk!"

"It's very good exercise, I'm told."

"But you can't leave me here. There's probably only one train a day."

"And who's to blame, old chum?" Pat asked sarcastically. "Get your pals in Parliament to pull their fingers out."

"It's not my pigeon. Look, just give me a lift up and..."

"Sorry, old chum." Pat cut him off. "Have to look after Number One."

He revved the engine. The car shot away, leaving the Minister in a cloud of dust – and too nettled to notice that it had not turned back towards London.

What is a Village Green?

A village green has been authoritatively described as an open space surrounded by houses or curtilages, and used for lawful sports or pastimes for a period of twenty years or more without protest or permission from the owner of the fee simple or the Lord of the Manor. The inhabitants of Longford Stanton had enjoyed sports and pastimes, lawful and unlawful, on their extensive stretch of greenery for more than a thousand years. Several ancient but well-preserved artefacts reminded visitors and residents alike of the central part it had played, and continued to play, in the life of the village. At the northern end a slender stone cross recalled the village's lost importance as a market centre. Facing this at the other, southern, end a cross of more modern date and design was dedicated to the glorious dead of two world wars. Local legend had it that this memorial occupied the site of a medieval gallows and, although scoffed at by one of the Reverend Breagh's predecessors, Rectors had been enlisted to bless the spot before its erection to ensure that memories of the heroes of Longford Stanton were not defiled by ghosts of its villains.

More tangible evidence of local law enforcement in the days of instant justice could be seen in a fenced-off area beside the duck pond. Here, under an old oak, were the stocks and whipping post, their worn creosoted woodwork reinforced with thick iron plates bolted to the uprights.

The centre portion of the green was carefully mown and rolled for the coming cricket season and the whole was surrounded by a jumble of shops and houses – the latter mostly built as labourers' cottages but now, with few exceptions, transformed into desirable residences for commuters to Bristol, Swindon and Gloucester living out a rural idyll of Olde England.

Here and there larger houses stood apart behind thick black railings on low walls or visible only through wrought-iron gates in higher walls. Between two of these residences a broadwalk led to a church of St Thomas the Doubter, its presence marked by the turrets of a square tower seen above the trees and roofs of the houses.

To the north of this broadwalk facing the duck pond across a wide cobbled forecourt was the Beak and Wedge Inn, its venerable half-timbered frontage wreathed in the twisted, tangled branches of an enormous wisteria. Although clearly Elizabethan in style it claimed much earlier origins, a claim reinforced by another local legend (Longford Stanton was rich in them) that Henry VIII had stood in the doorway and downed a pint of the local ale while watching the Abbot's head being removed on a block by the duck pond.

A more detailed version of this legend had it that blood

from the headless Abbot had spurted into the pond turning it a deep red – an event that recurred (it was alleged) every now and then on the anniversary of the ghastly deed. No one had ever witnessed this, but as the date of the original happening was uncertain there was room for argument as to its veracity. Others of a more practical mind had noted that on particular dates the sun sets directly at the end of the High Street and was reflected crimsonly in the pond.

Pat Pendle stood where Henry VIII had stood and eyed the heart of the village with a mixture of amusement and incredulity, embodying the inbred cynicism of a city sophisticate that such things could still be!

Once embarked on a seduction it was not Pat Pendle's nature to abandon it until victory had been achieved. Modern sexual mores being what they were his undoubted good looks, easy manner, and not least, his wealth, had so far kept his record unblemished – and he did not intend to have this fine progression of victories spoilt by a Rector's daughter. Perish the thought – the novelty of the challenge and Warwick Tewson's airy dismissal of his chance of success had whetted his appetite for the chase. This was something more than a simple matter of 'come round to my place for a nightcap!' The girl had standards. Therefore, on abandoning the Minister of Rural Affairs to the mercy of the rural railway, he had decided to see what opportunity there was of meeting Shelagh Breagh independently on her home ground.

From the steps of the Beak and Wedge, Longford Stanton had all the appearance of a dreamed-up setting for a film romance or melodrama. Take away the cars and one could almost expect maidens with flowers in their hair to come tripping out to dance at a maypole. It lay mellow and still in the afternoon sunlight, a bit of old England preserved in amber for commuters to play out their fantasies of rustic bliss. A waste tip, nuclear or otherwise, would give them a rude awakening. This bit of the garden that was England was likely to end up a compost heap.

Where No Virgin Says No

The room that the porter ushered him into carried the romantic dream of rural England still further. Like the reception area it had thick black beams and white walls with pretty chintz coverings on the solitary easy chair. A leaded window looked out over a car park to a patchwork of fields that rose to a skyline of rounded hills.

"Are those the famous Humps?" Pat asked the porter.

"That's 'em sir. Oh yes, that's 'em. That's the Humps."

"How did they get their name?"

"Oh that's interesting that is. Come to look over them, have you, sir? A lot do that. About the newts, that it?"

"Newts?"

"Famous for newts, the Humps. Folks come to see 'em. Would that be your line, sir?"

"Never mind my line. How did they come to be called Humps? Why not just hills?"

"Maidens' parts, sir. Humps is maidens' parts round here. Not now o' course, but one time. Yes. Maidens' parts." The porter moved to the window and pointed. "You imagine a maiden from a part'lar point of looking and there she is. Two buttocks being her bottom and two being her bosoms. Higher up, like."

"That's only four. There's five. That little one. What's that supposed to be? No, don't tell me, I can guess."

"Ah, thats it, sir, you're right. That's her pudden – the maiden's pudden, tho' mind, there is some call it the afters. With men always being after it. If you take my meaning, sir."

Pat took it. "You must have had rather randy

ancestors."

"We all like our greens, don't we, sir? They do say there's more maids become mothers on the Pudden than in their own beds. Famous for courting, it was. Ask any woman round here to go to the Pudden with you and her saying yes or no means yes or no all the way." The porter chuckled, throatily. "They do say as Henry number eight – him that knocked down the Abbey, not knowing how it was here, asked the Lady of the Manor to show him the Pudden and she fainted clean off. Right out. Haha! 'Tain't said what happened after. But things ent what they was here, not with all the incomers."

"What about the Rector? Is he an incomer?"

"Churchers down't count, do they? But he makes a noise in the village does the Rector. Thunnery good preacher he is. Better'n the telly. You should hear him telling 'em."

"I might do that," said Pat and flipped the man a coin. He felt it had been earned.

The porter thanked him and went away to make a telephone call. Ackers would be interested to know that the Humps had a visitor.

Ye and ff

The half a dozen shops that served the village were in a narrow street away from the Green. No effort had been spared to retain the ambience of rural England. Open sacks of cereal stood outside the grocer's, the window featured an ancient coffee grinder with coffee beans, artistically piled with careful carelessness – but a discreet notice informed the potential customer that a full range of freezer and convenience goods were stocked inside. The butcher's window sported game and fowls, the butcher himself a striped apron and a straw boater. In a brave attempt to sustain an ancient flavour the greengrocer and the confectioner traded their wares from behind facades which proclaimed the trade within an old cursive script, 'Ye' and 'ff' figuring prominently.

The ironmonger's displayed an old penny-farthing on the forecourt, the inevitable antique shops huddled together in a cobbled square off the shopping street. Here, tucked in a corner, Pat found a bookshop and bought a guide to the flora and fauna of the Humps. At the church (Saxon tower, late Norman doorway and porch, note stone seats to accommodate children and roughly carved cross believed to be made by a twelfth-century pilgrim; also Norman font and several Tudor tombs), Pat paid most attention to the times of services and concluded that Shelagh would probably attend communion at ten o'clock in the morning.

The Abbey ruins were protected by a locked gate but could be seen by appointment with the Rector. For a moment Pat toyed with the idea of doing this, but decided that a chance meeting in church would be better than presenting himself at the Rectory and expressing surprise at finding Shelagh there – if she happened to be. He did, however, take a glance at the home of his intended – well, no, victim was too strong a word...his...the object of his desire. That was about it.

The scouting mission accomplished he retired to the Beak and Wedge where he took an early dinner in the Carvery – Baron of English Beef with garden fresh vegetables and steamed pudding – and retired to study the books.

The historical preamble confirmed that the Humps had been a favourite haunt of courting couples, particularly the attractive area known as the Pudden. While he omitted the porter's ascription of the names, the writer hinted delicately that the decline in alfresco lovemaking was directly related to the growth in car ownership. This stirred

Pat's imagination. All his lovemaking had taken place indoors, except for one disastrous attempt at coupling in a swimming pool on a hot night in St Lucia. Sex under a blue sky amid buttercups and daisies, presumably how it all started, was a delight he felt he ought to experience. He turned to the main text with anticipation, the elements of a campaign beginning to form in his mind. A reference or two to the habits of the warty newt, an expression of admiration for the ganny orchid and other rarities of nature would persuade Shelagh Breagh to walk with him over the Humps to inspect their habitat and, with a modicum of luck, pause awhile on the Pudden!

Unhappy Homecoming

Warwick Tewson's arrival at his home in Longford Stanton could not be described as a happy one. He had walked the mile to the Wether Blewitt station only to find there were no trains, the Saturday service having been discontinued as unprofitable following privatisation. Sweating his way back to the pub he had called down a fine selection of imprecations on Pat's head for deserting him, and an equal number on the PM's for sins of a more ideological nature.

A taxi from the pub to Swindon had entailed an hour's wait, only to arrive at the station as the train to Longford Proper – the one at Longford Stanton having been closed completely following privatisation – was disappearing up the track. A further delay of almost two hours had done nothing to improve his temper. By the time a second taxi, from Longford Proper to Longford Stanton, had deposited him on his doorstep he was in no mood for wifely chiding.

Sylvia tried to be understanding, but her understanding was stretched to breaking point. Not only had she prepared the yellow bedroom for the expected guest – (did he know what a back-breaking uncomfortable job that was?) – she had also invited Shelagh Breagh to dinner and prepared a menu for four. Why hadn't he rung back and told her it was all off? Then at least she could have let Shelagh know.

Irritated beyond diplomacy Warwick said she could start dismantling the bloody bedroom because soon they wouldn't need it as he was selling the house. Why? Because there was a rumour that Pitts' field might be used as a tip...nothing serious, he added hastily, just a tip of some sort...household rubbish...besides which property prices were peaking so now was a good time to get out at a profit. And there was no point in her arguing, his mind was made up and for God's sake keep your mouth shut or we'll lose money I can't afford and my seat as well because it's an Official Secret. Sylvia was incredulous – why would a tip be secret?

"Commercial confidentiality," her husband snapped, "under the Freedom of Information Act. And I'm going to bath. I'm whacked."

Over dinner Warwick lied vigorously in answer to Shelagh's questions about the ailments of the absent guest and proclaimed his regret at having to lose the Breagh family as neighbours. Unfortunately the house was too big for just two of them and inconvenient in other ways. A burden for Sylvia, who remained uncomfortably silent until Shelagh's departure when she bitterly censured him for making her a party to his lies. In an attempt to mollify her Warwick suggested bed and bit of "the old roly-poly".

Sylvia threw his pyjamas at him and told him to enjoy himself in the yellow bedroom.

Despite it all Warwick spent a reasonably untroubled night. He had married Sylvia for practical reasons of policy. Putting up with her, he had to admit, rare tantrums was the price he had to pay for it. Were he to give her his real reason for selling the house things would be easier, but he couldn't risk it.

The really bitter pill was that not one of his chums in Whitehall had dropped him the slightest hint of what was going on – they must have known; the decision couldn't have been a sudden one. It would have been mulled over, discussed, planned...and part of the bloody plan must have been making sure he didn't know. So much for the loyalty of friends! The blasted Freedom of Information Act shouldn't be used against pals.

But he had beaten the buggers. At least he was pretty sure he had. Pendle had been put out, no doubt about that, but the Dorset gravel contract was a very lucrative sweetener – no contractor in his right mind would risk losing it! A telephone call confirming its availability would do the trick and delay the start of the infill.

Warwick yawned and turned to sleep. Sylvia would be more conciliatory at breakfast. With all her faults she was a realist.

Her initial greeting at the breakfast table was silence which reassured him and, it being Sunday, Warwick's mind was dwelling on the glimpse he would get of Shelagh Breagh's dorsal attractions. The Tewson pew was immediately behind that occupied by the Rector's wife and daughter. This happy arrangement provided him with an intimate study of Shelagh Breagh's rear while she was kneeling, sitting or standing according to the rituals of the service her father was conducting. How Sylvia would have reacted had she known the erotic fantasies her husband was toying with it was impossible to tell. Her thoughts were on more practical matters. As she broke her egg, she said, "What about Shelagh's newts?"

"Eh?" said Warwick, rapidly refocusing his mind from Shelagh's buttocks. "What?"

"Will this tip affect the red-speckled newts Shelagh looks after?"

"It's...they're on the Humps, not Pitts' field."

"That's next to the Humps."

"So what?"

"There's bound to be an outcry from the conservationists. They'll expect you to do something."

Warwick activated his defensive reflexes. "It is not the responsibility of my department."

"You are Minister of Rural Affairs."

"The infill...tip...is a problem for the Ministry of Development. It also comes within the Freedom of Information Act so conservationists can scream their heads off. It can't be talked about."

"The Information Act has nothing to do with newts surely," said Sylvia tartly. "They're fauna, and definitely a Rural Affair. You're bound to be asked about them."

"The newts are on the Humps and the Humps have nothing to do with my department. If I bring it up Fawkes of Development will simply refuse to discuss it."

"But when they start on Pitts the press will be interested and..."

"The media won't be allowed to mention it – they can't even say it's forbidden by the Act because that's forbidden too! I've told you plain enough, national security and commercial confidence are involved. It's top secret. Tell anyone and my career's finished. Remember that."

"What is the point of making anything secret when you can't hide what's going on? At least everyone round here will know exactly what's going on."

Warwick deemed it unwise to reveal what he had learned from Pat Pendle about the nuclear aspect of the problem. Sylvia might turn even more awkward. So he changed the subject.

"I meant to ask you," he said, "did you know that Paula Pomfrey is a les?"

"Is a what?"

"A lesbian, and her partner in the action is Pendle's sister. According to him they're sharing beds at Stoke Kirby. I wonder if Sir Archie knows? If he does I bet his old school tie is curling round the edges."

Sylvia stared. "Are you serious?"

"Never more so. He says his brother's gay too. Jesus! Must be some family. Thank God we're normal."

Sylvia said nothing but continued to stare at him.

"Aren't you surprised? Can you imagine it? Paula Pomfrey rolling round in bed with another woman enjoying a bit of whatdoyouthink!"

"I've always liked Paula," said Sylvia, and resumed eating her egg.

Virgin Take Care

When Maggie Williams discovered that Pat Pendle had gone to spend a few days in the country her suspicions were immediately aroused, but it was not till the Sunday morning that she telephoned Shelagh at the Rectory and discovered that her intuition had been partly right. Puzzled by Shelagh's news that Pat had been detained in town by some mysterious ailment she promised to investigate and report. She also advised Shelagh to be on her guard: if Pat Pendle was making for Longford Stanton it would not be to enjoy the country air. It was the Kooh-in-Noor to a Brazil nut he was on a deflowering expedition, and Shelagh was probably the flower he intended to 'de'.

"For the honour of our sex," pleaded Maggie, "give him the air! Leave me at least one female friend who hasn't seen him with his socks off."

Shelagh assured her that there was no danger. When she walked up the aisle she would be in white, and the white was going to be a true symbol of maidenhood. But when she dashed out to attend morning service – Maggie's call having delayed her – there was an odd little hope in her heart that it was something other than the pursuit of her body that might bring Pat Pendle to Longford Stanton. Of course if it was true and he was well...morally loose...as Maggie believed, then he needed to be taught that women had not been created solely for his enjoyment. On the other hand, somewhere inside, she knew not why or where, she entertained a faint hope that he was not entirely the sexual predator he'd been painted. And men did change, or could be persuaded to.

Had Pat Pendle been privy to her thoughts he would have fled from Longford Stanton with all possible speed. A desirable female with a missionary zeal for matrimony is a bachelor's nemesis.

CHAPTER FOUR

Wine that is Water

The Reverend Donald Breagh's favourite reading was the Book of Job. Constant study of this great work of wail and woe and salvation had convinced him that in modern times it closely reflected the parson's lot. Once again the Lord was allowing Satan to walk up and down the earth, denying good men the prosperity evident among sinners. His own situation was proof of this. By investing the bulk of his fortunes in Blinders, Block & Adams' High Return Overseas Gilt Fund, he had fallen for Satan's wiles. In the collapse of that House of Mammon the City was revealed as the maw of hell, wherein sat Satan dangling easy profit as bait to tempt innocents to enter and be consumed.

At the time it had seemed a wise move. When the Royal Peculiar preferment had fallen to him he had been pretty firmly hedged about financially. But during the years of his tenure inflation had devastated the hedge somewhat, allowing the chill winds of depreciation to blow round the Rector's income. The glossy, unsolicited brochure from Blinders, Block & Adams offering a two and a half per cent increase in investment income was too attractive to be ignored. Assured by advisers that there was no risk involved – the fund was in Gilts, the firm licensed by the Department of Trade and given a clean bill by its financial watchdogs – he had plunged confidently in, removed his capital from the dull, stingy security of several building societies and pitched it into the High Return Overseas Gilt Fund. Eighteen months later the brochure had become a tinselled whore of Babylon. Mr Blinders was nowhere to be found, the High Return Gilts Overseas Fund had sunk without trace and the Rector was on his beam ends with only his income from the preferment to survive on.

His one hope now was that his suffering would eventually be rewarded by elevation to a bishopric, but in the meantime it annoyed him that many of his parishioners still enjoyed their Chateau Lafite while he had to endure the dubious wines of Stanton Proper supermarkets. It annoyed him further that some of them were the very professionals who had lured him into the maw of Mammon. Others, he knew, were of the same ilk, financing their pleasures not by honest toil but by shuffling bits of paper hither and thither, formulating deals that he suspected were not quite moral, whereas his comparative poverty was the outcome of his dedication to comforting the sick, etcetera, and trying to explain the ways of God to Man – a task he had long concluded was beyond him.

In short the Reverend was becoming more and more aware that there was something wrong in the way that the worldly system of rewards was arranged and, because he was an honest man, he had to admit that a tiny sliver of doubt niggled at his previously unquestioning faith in the wisdom of the Lord. Wisely, he kept his tiny doubt deep within his being, never allowing it to surface for closer inspection but, as is the way with believers, the more his doubt niggled, the more dogmatic his sermons became, and the more he suffered the supermarket non-vintages, the fiercer his condemnation of the fleshy appetites of his flock.

On the night that Pat Pendle was enjoying, with his Baron of Beef, a full-bodied, nosy Burgundy (reasonably priced at £9.95), before settling down to the habits and habitat of the red-speckled warty newt, Mrs Breagh, in the interest of domestic economy, placed on the Rectory dinner table a particularly foul *vin ordinaire* – this week's bargain buy at £3.60 a giant litre bottle. The Rector retired in disgust to his study to vent his frustration in the composition of a sermon of such virulence that, had he delivered it verbatim, it would almost certainly have resulted in his being defrocked. Fortunately second thoughts prevailed. On Sunday morning when he climbed into the pulpit it was a severely edited version that he placed on his reading desk.

When describing the Rector's preaching as "thunnery" the porter at the Beak and Wedge had not exaggerated. What he failed to mention was the Rector's habit of sweeping his congregation with a slow, menacing gaze before launching into his rhetoric, as if threatening with instant damnation those foolish enough to imagine that they were going to escape unscathed, with their sins intact.

Seated at the back of the church Pat Pendle marvelled that a face capable of such expressive menace could have had a part in creating such a beauty as Shelagh. His plan had been to arrive early, hang about the porch and exchange surprised greetings when she arrived to worship the Lord.

'Good Lord, what are you doing down here?' she'd say.

'I've heard there are some interesting newts on the Humps,' would be his response.

'You mean the great warty?'

'That's it exactly. Fascinating creature. *Triturus cristatus*, if I'm lucky enough to get a glimpse of one. They're my favourite amphibian – though they mate on land actually.'

'Really?'

'Oh yes...I'm crazy about them. Silly, I suppose...'

'Nonsense, of course it's not silly. I'm crazy about them myself.'

'You're joking!'

'No, I'm not. I can show you where to find them if you like.'

'That's very kind – but I don't want to put you out, take up your time.'

'For a fellow newt fan, it's a pleasure. When shall we meet?'

From then on it should be plain sailing. Over the Humps and, with luck, a bit of dilly-dallying on the Pudden!

Unfortunately the Burgundy and a long session on the local flora and fauna caused him to oversleep. Arriving late at the church he had found it well attended – Sunday church in the village being part of the rural idyll, particularly a church with royal connections – and the Rector's sermons, centring of late on the evils of pursuing worldly wealth, informed the incomers with a pleasurable masochistic guilt, while the locals felt virtuously that the increase in the value of their houses was fortuitous and therefore the strictures did not concern them. The usher guided him to a seat at the back, giving him no chance to walk the aisles for a glimpse of Shelagh.

"I take as my text," the Rector announced threateningly, "verse 40 from the Second Book of Kings. *'And it came to pass that they were eating of the pottage when a man cried out, "Oh thou man of God, there is death in the pot!"'*"

The Rector paused impressively, then repeated the important bit, slowly, "'There is death in the pot!'", before launching into his homily. "Ah, what pot, my friends? What pot? And how did it come about that true believers – men of God – found death in it? And who was the man of

God they cried to? Brethren, it was Elisha! Elisha told men to make pottage in a great pot for their well-being – but in the pot they put the wild gourd the colocynth! Ooooh, the colocynth is pretty, brethren! The colocynth is round and smooth like the sweet honey melon. The colocynth charms the eye with its prettiness. It makes the taste buds water, tempting the teeth to sink themselves in its fleshy promise! But like the great whore who sitteth upon the waters arrayed in scarlet and gold and precious stones – she who has tempted the kings of the earth to commit fornication – like her, the colocynth tempts only to destroy. Eat it," continued the Rector, suddenly abandoning his old Testament rhetoric in favour of plain English, "and you get a severe attack of the gripes. They gathered colocynth for the pot expecting a nice, nourishing plate of pottage but got instead a plateful of powerful astringent and thought they were dying! Why did they do it? Why did they put colocynth in the pot instead of nourishing herbs?" The Rector leaned back and surveyed his listeners with an accusing eye. "Because they were ignorant! Because they were weak! They judged worth by looks! They fell for the label on the bottle! That is how Satan works, my friends. Like the great whore and the colocynth, he puts on his finery! Like the label of a bad bottle of wine it tempts you to buy and rewards you with stomach trouble...er...yes..."

The Rector shuffled his papers to sort out his metaphors. Pat scanned the heads before him and finally fixed on one that was familiar. It was Bridget. He saw her face distinct in profile as she turned to whisper something to her companion, a pale-faced female with busy red hair. Paula Pomfrey! Pat drew a breath of annoyance. As soon as they saw him – and they were bound to if he loitered to find Shelagh – Paula would fall on his neck demanding to know, with her great horsey laugh, what he was doing away from the fleshpots. Any chance of appearing before

Shelagh as an innocent searcher after the habitat of the warty newt was doomed.

"What", boomed the Rector, resuming his rhetorical style, "is the answer? The answer, my friends, is to watch what you put in the pot! Do not be deceived by the gaudy lusts of the flesh – gather to yourself only good deeds to nourish the pottage of Faith. Spiritual food! Remember the widow – give to those in need – do not permit yourselves to enjoy what others have not, and remember too that the collection boxes are at the West Door as you leave. Let us now sing 'Oh God, keep me not in hunger please'."

The congregation rose with a great shuffling. Pat slipped quickly out. The Rector was welcome to his nourishing pot – Pat preferred gaudy lust – and a new way would have to be found to meet the object of his fleshy desire.

He did not have to find a way. As he left the church she was coming through the lychgate. A picture of natural beauty, lightsome of step, bright of eye and face aglow. Pat's heart turned over.

"Hello!" he said, as she approached.

"Hello," she replied with a smile and walked straight past him into the church.

As she took her seat in the pew at the back and joined in the singing her heart was pounding. It had taken all her self-control to treat Pat Pendle as a stranger. Would he now ignore her?

It's Only Worth It If You Don't Have It.

"A very large gin and tonic, sir?"

"A very large one!"

"Yes, sir," said the porter, who apparently doubled as the barman. "Got you down, did it?"

"Eh?"

"It's like that with the first-timers, sir. But don't you

get worried – it don't last. Would you want ice, sir?"

Pat shook his head. He had never understood the passion for destroying the flavour of drinks with ice, and he had even hesitated for a moment over the tonic. His ego had received such a battering that he doubted if anything short of an intravenous injection of alcohol, or some other morale booster, could possibly restore its equilibrium. The bloody woman hadn't even recognised him!

In London, in select resorts of the world, he was accustomed to instant recognition and welcome. His company was sought, cultivated, cherished, yet here was some country bumpkin of a parson's daughter who, despite enjoying his undivided attention at the Williams' soirée, had walked past him without so much as a flicker of interest or recognition. It was so humiliating he found it hard to believe it had actually happened!

"What it is, sir," said the porter, putting the drink on the bar and interrupting Pat's mental flagellation, "is guilt – oh yes...we're all guilty – dearie me, and the Rector knows it." The porter leaned forward confidentially and lowered his voice. "Cos he's guilty himself! Parsons didn't ought to live off the fat of the land. They should suffer with the people. That'll be two pound twenty, sir."

Pat paid. Guilt was a feeling he had never experienced, at least not in his adult life, and he saw no reason why living off the fat of the land should engender it.

"You're talking a lot of old rope," he told the porter. "What's the point of suffering if you don't have to?"

"Dearie me, sir, that is the point. It's only worth doing it if you don't have to. That way you can enjoy it – like they had this doing without lunch in the church for the starving somewhere. Wonderful it went, wonderful – half the village turned out for it. They were in here afterwards happy as saints on a feast day. We did so well the boss tried to get them to fix another. Only his daughter put a stop to it."

"Whose daughter?"

"Rector's, of course. She said if the boss was that keen he could donate all his profits that day to charity. Put him off, that did." The porter chuckled appreciatively – clearly he had enjoyed his employer's discomfiture. "Oh yes, dearie me, there's no fooling her! She's sharp!"

"Really." Pat did not have to feign interest. He wanted to know more about this Rector's daughter who had passed him by as if he were nothing but an animated bit of the scenery. "Is she liked in the village?"

"Depends who by, but generally yes, tho' – " the porter looked round carefully and lowered his voice still further, "not by some. There's some say she's socialist."

"I've been told she's a green," said Pat, to whom all political parties were anathema. "A conservationist."

"Oh she is that, sir, oh yes – very hot she is on round here, works for them preserving things, specially round the Humps... Oh, dearie me...yes. And here they come. The worshippers!"

A crowd of people surged into the bar. The churchgoers of Longford Stanton and its environs required more than spiritual sustenance to survive the rigours of the Sabbath. Pat turned back to his drink as the barman moved away and in the mirror behind the bar he saw an unmistakable clump of red hair pushing its way to the bar. In a moment Paula Pomfrey would be beside him.

He ducked his head, slid quietly off the stool and, keeping his back to the approaching horde, went into the gentlemen's toilet, conveniently situated in the wall most distant from the street door.

A short, stocky man was about his business in the urinal furthest from the door. On Pat's entrance he looked round, displaying a face that resembled an autumnal leaf that had been lately attacked by wireworm.

"Good running ale this," he said. "Makes you run!"

Pat made a vague noise of assent and pretended to apply himself to the task for which the room was designed. The stocky man evidently considered it a good place for philosophical exposition of the merits or otherwise of ale on the human plumbing system.

"Banster's Bitter's the worst. In one end and out the other before you've a chance to enjoy it – waste of good money ent it?"

Receiving nothing more than the flicker of a smile in response to this libellous observation on Longford Stanton's local brew he challenged Pat with a direct, searching question.

"Not from round here are you?"

"No."

"On a visit?"

Pat nodded. The man stepped back from the urinal and adjusted himself with a convulsive jerk.

"Staying long?"

"No."

"Just doing a bit of business, eh?"

"Sort of."

"To do with the Humps, is it?"

Pat glanced at him sharply. The man grinned, showing several gaps where teeth should have been.

"Oh I know something's going on there," he said. "I don't miss much round here. I've seen 'em at it."

"At what?"

"Pokin' about – specially round the Pudden. Makin' out they'm ramblers, but that sort don't go pokin' in the ground – and that's what they've been doing. Pokin' in the ground – so what's going on, eh?"

Pat abandoned his attempt to make water and zipped up his flies. The Ministry's inspection of the site hadn't gone unnoticed after all!

"Perhaps they're looking for oil," he said, inviting a denial in the hope that it would reveal the extent of local knowledge and conjecture.

"You don't look for oil on hills."

"No, I suppose not. But what else could it be?"

"I'm asking you."

A large man in tweeds came in and went immediately about his business, glancing at Pat and the man as he did so.

"What's this Ackers? A conference?"

"Just welcoming a visitor," said the man identified as Ackers. "Making him feel at home."

"Oh yes." The newcomer twisted his head and inspected Pat's carefully selected, casual clothes. "Not one of them, are you?"

"If I were," said Pat brutally, "I'd have to be pretty desperate to fancy you!"

Ackers chortled. The tweedy man spluttered.

"You're being damned insolent!"

"I don't like fat scuttlebutts who shop in cottages."

The man's neck bulged. His face purpled. "I'll have the law on you, and you, Ackers. It's still a crime to carry on your sort of game in public. You'll suffer for this. Both of you."

"Great," said Ackers cheerfully. "I'll tell 'em you made approaches to me and tried to touch me up. He's my witness," he indicated Pat, "that you offered me 50p for a bit of backgammon but I turned you down as it is rumoured that you have not been using condoms."

The man shook himself, tugged at his flies and went out without a word.

"A well known grubber called Pitts and known as the Pitts," said Ackers. "Nobody likes him." He turned at the door. "You coming?"

"You go," said Pat. "I'll stay here for a bit."

"Stay here?"

"That's what I said."

Ackers eyed him doubtfully. Pat laughed. The exchange with Pitts had engendered a feeling of comradeship.

"There's someone in the bar I don't want to meet. This was the nearest bolt-hole."

"A she?"

Pat nodded.

"Ah, well," said Ackers. "That I can understand. You're a fellow victim. Any man escaping from a woman gets my help and guidance. Come on, we can get out this way."

The toilet was illuminated by an opaque window. Ackers fiddled with the catch and pushed it open.

They scrambled out into a cobbled yard. Ackers led the way through to the front of the Inn, facing the Green. "If you go in," he said, "you'll be seen from the bar."

This had already occurred to Pat. One of the features of the Beak and Wedge was its large reception area, which served both as a residents' lounge and bar, the only division being large glass panels framed in oak. It was impossible to reach the reception desk and stairs without the risk of being seen.

"I'll walk round a bit," he told Ackers. "Wait till the coast is clear."

"How'll you know when it is?"

"She won't be drinking all day."

"Describe her to me and I'll nip in and see if she's still there."

This did not appeal to Pat. He guessed that Ackers was as intent on satisfying his curiosity as he was on helping and he did not want to reveal his connection with Paula Pomfrey or Bridget.

"I'll walk about a bit," he said. "Thanks for your help."

He started to walk off but Ackers followed him.

"Don't trust me, eh?" he said.

Pat stopped. "Look," he said. "There's no way I'm going to let you find out who the woman is, so stop trying, okay?"

"I like that. I like that," said Ackers. "Straight from the shoulder, and right to! Right. Married is she? Must be."

"It's got nothing to do with sex."

Ackers gave a guffaw of disbelief.

"It's true."

"Anything to do with a woman is to do with sex. Can't help it being how we're made, more's the pity. Here, tell you what. You come home with me. No no," he continued when Pat resisted, "No tricking. It'll help you."

Ackers led Pat to a row of four tiny cottages facing the Beak and Wedge across the Green.

"Incomers 'ud like to lay their hands on these," he said. "They want it all Noddy in Toyland an' the grass cut with nail scissors. So we keep these mucky just to rile 'em."

He opened the gate in a wicket fence at the end cottage. The front garden was a small patch of grass on one side of a weedy path to the front door, barely half a dozen paces from the gate. Like the grass, the paintwork of the cottages needed attention. Both wore a look of quiet despair, contrasting strongly with the neatly groomed others round the Green. The brass door knob was bright only from use and hung from too large a hole, lacking a backplate.

Ackers pushed open the cottage door and went inside. Pat followed. There was no hall. They were immediately in a small room in which a shiny old rexine three-piece suite draped with antimacassars took up most of the space. It was tightly arranged around a shaggy oblong rug which fronted a small iron fireplace. In one corner a bamboo stand carried a brass pot. A similar stand in another corner bore what appeared to be a coloured bust of Queen Victoria. In the wall opposite the street was another door which, presumably, led to the kitchen.

"Only two up and two down," said Ackers, answering Pat's unspoken thoughts. "But if you sit here," he indicated the arm of one of the rexine chairs nearest to the lace-curtained window, "you'll be able to see everyone who leaves the Beak and know when the coast is clear. All right?"

Pat started to protest but Ackers cut him short.

"I'm leaving you, shan't be watching. It's a payback for putting the Pitts in his place. You'll have to move the lace a bit but..." He suited the action to the words, then stopped and peered through the window towards the Beak and Wedge. "Well, there's a thing...don't usually see her at the Beak."

"Who?"

"Rector's daughter. Her in the woollen outfit. If I was your age I'd be after her – not as I'd have much chance – my class. And she ent easy loosed up either, like young wimmen these days who'll take a man to bed like they'd a hot bottle in winter...no, not her... Barmy, o'course, but a good 'un."

Pat looked at him sharply. "Barmy? How d'you mean?

"One of these green 'uns. You know, all eating nuts and don't tread on the daisies." Ackers dropped the curtain back into place. "But give her her due – she thinks of ordinary folk as well. Wouldn't be her you're hiding from, would it?

"As a matter of fact," said Pat, seeing an opportunity to establish his credentials, "I'm here to take a look at the habitat of the rare red-speckled *Triturus cristatus* warty newt."

In return he got a look of incredulity followed by a bellow of laughter.

"Hahaha! Lord a'mighty!" Ackers slapped Pat on the back and made for the door. "You watch out for your lady."

"No, you wait! Hang on – what's so funny?"

"Look." Ackers leaned on the doorpost, his autumnal face resuming its normal expression of foxy amiability. "I ain't no saint – only thing I do straight is speak my mind – anyone here will tell you that – they know me, I've lived here all my life. Since I was a lad I've seen all sorts clambering over the Humps looking for everything from the ganny orchid to the lesser fried fritillary and – long 'uns, short 'uns, fat 'uns, thin 'uns, man, woman and every hand out in between – but if you're one of 'em I'm the Resurrection of the Lord and life everlasting!"

"Then get ready to make water into wine. I am definitely interested in the habitat of the rare red-speckled warty newt."

"I don't believe you."

"Why not? Why shouldn't I be interested in the newt?" said Pat loftily. "This fascinating amphibian mates on scrub land but lays its eggs in water. The Humps is one of the few places in the country favourable to its continuance as the area has ample supplies of the succulent white-ended worm which is the only item of its diet. There! See? Would I know all that if I wasn't interested in warty newts?"

"You haven't said anything about its legs."

"What?"

"Its legs...there is something funny about the red-speckled warty's legs that makes it different to other newts. What is it?"

Pat paused. He examined Ackers' face. The leaf mould countenance gave nothing away but he sensed a trap.

"It's not something you'd forget," said Ackers, pre-empting any excuse. "There is one funny thing about the red-speckled warties that every newt-lover knows." He paused, awaiting an answer. "You tell me what it is and I'll believe you're interested in newts."

"I can't see", said Pat, having run through the previous night's study in an attempt to remember any reference to newts' legs, "that it matters whether you believe me or not."

"What you mean is, you don't know it's got six legs instead of the usual four."

"You're joking." Pat couldn't suppress a laugh. "Must be."

"But you don't know whether I am or not, do you?" Ackers left the door and came back to beside the chair. "Why not come out with it? All you know about newts is what you've read in that book Casey Harris wrote. You came out with it pretty well word for word."

Pat surrendered. There was no point in sustaining the fiction that he was a newt-worshipper, but he could not hide a twinge of irritation at being outwitted.

"All right, so I'm not an expert on newts. What's it to you?"

"What else you might be an expert in," said Ackers. "But it don't really work out. You hide out in the gents so a woman won't see you. Then you start making out you're nutty on newts when it's as plain as a bull's bollocks you don't even know what it's like to get your feet wet. So what's it add up to? What sort of sense does it make?"

"You tell me," said Pat. "And why are you so keen to work it out anyway?"

Ackers lowered himself into a corner of the settee and stared speculatively at Pat, who turned away at the window. Outside the Beak and Wedge a small knot of people surrounded Warwick Tewson, and even at a distance it was plain that the Minister of Rural Affairs was not enjoying himself. Pat wondered if news of the proposed infill had already leaked out and if he was witnessing the first protests.

"Avoiding a woman I can understand," said Ackers, whose own speculations had kept him quiet for a while.

"I've spent time doing that myself. You like 'em, lay 'em, and then it's a matter of getting away from 'em. But newts! Only thing that can be is some sort of cover for you wanting to poke about on the Humps without too many questions being asked."

"Asked about what?"

"What you're up to. There have been others up there doing things. I've seen 'em through my bins but when I got there – well, they shifted quick when they saw me coming. So what was they up to, eh?"

Pat had more than an idea but did not intend to get involved. "Perhaps you should ask your local MP," he said. "He's over there."

Outside the Beak and Wedge the group was breaking up.

"If I asked him the time of day," said Ackers, "he'd want to know what was in it for him."

It was an accurate summing up of Tewson's character. Pat's incipient warming to Ackers rose a point.

"It looks like the ladies have been grilling him over something."

"I've heard he's selling his house. And they'll be wanting to know why he's leaving, shouldn't wonder. Good riddance, I say...but his wife's a good 'un. Deserves better, and her dad, he was a gent. Honest as the day was long. Don't get politicians like him nowadays. Bastards!" Ackers spat accurately into the fireplace. "Your lady, she gone yet?"

"Must have, I think."

"Don't you know?"

"You've been occupying my attention," said Pat.

Actually he'd been thinking that if Shelagh Breagh was an expert on newts she'd probably see through his pretence even quicker than Ackers. So the tactic needed reconsidering, more study perhaps.

"This damned newt hasn't really got six legs, has it?" he asked.

Ackers laughed. "Don't ask me. I've never seen one. But if it's women you want to know about, just ask."

Pat hesitated but, for once, resisted temptation.

Oh Jesus Misses the Redeeming Feature

If Pat Pendle's morning had been disappointing, Warwick Tewson's had been irritating and uncomfortable. Shelagh was not at morning service. Instead of the enchantment of her sylph-like rear, he had been confronted by the tweedy bulk of Paula Pomfrey. Adaptable as his erotic fantasies were, they remained resolutely unaroused by the square shoulders and broad hips of Sir Archibald's daughter. Her companion looked more promising but as she was directly in front of his wife a close examination of her attractions was impossible, but he wondered vaguely if she was Pendle's sister. It seemed unlikely as she was almost extravagantly feminine.

Leaving the church he'd been accosted by an elderly constituent who had enquired in a loud voice if it was true what he'd heard, that Tewson was selling up and leaving Longford Stanton. The question was put in the hearing of several other locals and aroused considerable curiosity.

During the planning controversy over Pitts field Warwick had assured his listeners in ringing tones that he was committed to conservation. As long as he was Minister of Rural Affairs speculators would never be allowed to despoil the treasured beauties of England's green and pleasant land – and certainly not that in the region of Longford Stanton!

It was a declaration that now hung like a millstone round his neck. Questions about the sale of his house, which he parried by claiming it was rather larger than he and Sylvia required, inevitably led to questions about just what the man with the dirty Rolls had been doing in Pitts field. Warwick assured them that no Planning Application had been received, and if one were, they had his word that it would be rejected out of hand.

Fortunately no one mentioned the Humps. It was Pitts field that his questioners saw as the potential threat to their carefully protected haven of rural bliss.

Throughout her husband's inquisition Sylvia had maintained a supportive silence, nodding and smiling whenever he turned to her for confirmation of what she knew were blatant lies. It was part of the lot of being a politician's wife that she detested most, not least because Warwick took it for granted that she agreed with his lies, as if her involvement in his deceptions was an integral part of their relationship, like sex. Something he was entitled to, and her participation in it should be automatic and unquestioning. Similarly, on returning from church, it was taken for granted that she would prepare lunch while Warwick entertained himself with the Sunday papers and a large gin and tonic on the terrace, weather permitting.

But on this particular Sunday it was not weather that kept him from the terrace. He was racked with anxiety – like a man forced against his will to cross a deep and deadly ravine by way of a rickety wooden bridge while suspecting that unseen enemies were hacking away at the supports; he needed reassurance, and sought it where a man had a right to find it. While his wife occupied herself with preparing lunch he occupied her ears with an analysis of the situation.

"Whatever we do it's going to look as if we're were hiding something."

"You are," said Sylvia, pointedly.

"We'll have to take the first offer we get – and Marston'll have to hurry," Warwick went on, ignoring her point with instinctive political pusillanimity. "Get the place off our hands before they start filli...tipping."

Sylvia said nothing but peeled a potato with deliberate care.

"I must get onto Pendle tomorrow," Warwick resumed moodily. "Get this starting date settled. The trouble is his sister. I don't suppose she's anything to do with the firm but she might know something and let it slip to Sir Archibald. Then we'd really be in the shit."

Sylvia was remembering how Bridget Pendle had squeezed her hand when they parted outside the church.

Peculiar, Very

"It seems very peculiar to me," said Mrs Breagh. "He's always been very proud of that house, and Sylvia loves it. Why is he selling it?"

"It's too big for them. You heard him say so."

"They've been there years without complaining. Why is it too big so suddenly?"

"I cannot read the man's mind," said the Rector impatiently. "And will you please sit still. I am trying to read."

"The ring must be here somewhere. However hard she threw it, it could not have gone out of the room."

The Rector sighed. "As you already turned the room over a hundred times you are hardly likely to find it under the hearth rug."

"It could have lodged in the weave. If I walk on it carefully with my shoes off I should feel it."

Mrs Breagh took off her shoes to put her theory into practice. Her husband folded his paper and was about to launch into a homily on losing and finding when his daughter entered the room dressed for outdoors.

"I'm going to the H..." she began, but stopped on

seeing her mother carefully pacing the rug. "Is something the matter with your feet?"

"I am trying to find the ring you threw at poor Andr..."

"Oh mother, for heaven's sake! It's not your business and it's over and done with anyway."

"I'm sure if you spoke to Andrew..."

"I'm going out. I'll be back for tea."

Shelagh went out quickly, slamming the door. The room shook.

"The girl has your temper," said Mrs Breagh. "We shall suffer for it."

"You must let her solve her own problems in her own way."

"She is our problem too," retorted his wife. "There's no real future for her in this environment thing she's doing."

"It is doing good community work and it interests her. Would you rather she were slaving in an office?"

"I would rather she got a husband. It would give her security."

"That may well be. But she does not have to confine her choice to the Hawkins family. There will be others in time, no doubt."

"Not as wealthy as the Hawkins."

"Money is not always a sure foundation of happiness," said the Rector, not without effort.

"And Mr Hawkins", said Mrs Breagh, "is, among other things, a wine importer."

"Hurrup," said the Rector.

Exploring the Pudden

To reach the Humps by foot from the centre of Longford Stanton it is necessary to cross the lane leading to the Rectory and follow a marked path that skirts one side of Pitts field to a broader path. Shaded by chestnuts, oaks, ash and a scattering of wild, purple-flowered rhododendrons this broader path curves round to the top of a hillock known as Little Tuppet. From here the village can be seen in its entirety – a cluster of rust-coloured roofs surrounding the tower of St Thomas the Doubter and the ruins of the Abbey, amid green and brown fields. A picture postcard idyll of peace and tranquillity, the only sign of modernity the distant white of the motorway snaking eastwards and westwards in and out of the undulating countryside. Here, like thousands before him, Pat Pendle paused to admire the view and recover his breath.

After leaving Ackers' cottage he had taken a light lunch and considered his next move. His first inclination had been to revert to his original idea of knocking on the Rectory door and asking to be shown the Abbey ruins. If Shelagh didn't recognise him then the coincidence element that had caused him originally to reject this plan was no obstacle. Unfortunately Sunday, being a heavy working day for the Rector, was one of the days when he was not available to conduct visitors around the ruins and regale them with the details of Henry's dark misconduct.

It then occurred to him that good generals always reconnoitre the terrain over which they intend to campaign, the object being to select a site that made resistance impractical and victory a certainty. Then, having manoeuvred the enemy there, graciously accept her surrender.

Fired by the positive nature of this approach his next consideration was what to wear. Exploring the depths of rural England on foot was not a factor he had taken into account when selecting his wardrobe. Physical activity, other than that of the bedroom, having no place in his lifestyle, what leisurewear he possessed was geared towards more sedentary pursuits. However, it was a fine day, warm and sunny, the ground dry underfoot, so there was really no problem. He chose a pair of storm-grey Gaultier slacks, a Benkerman print shirt and cable-stitch, burnt-orange sweater, finishing off the ensemble with patterned socks and his brown leather, hand-lasted Timmerber shoes. Cushioned insoles made them ideal for walking. Thus equipped, and quite pleased with his appearance, he set out on his exploration of the Humps – receiving helpful hints as to the best route from the slightly bemused porter of the Beak and Wedge.

The air was fresh, a light breeze cooled the heat of the afternoon as, having recovered his breath from the ascent, he turned again to the path which descended the other side of the Little Tuppet through a steep-sided gully towards the Humps proper.

"It's a bit up and downy till you get clear of Tuppet," the porter had said. "Oh dearie me, yes. But once you get through the gully it's sweet walking."

A lover of nature would have delighted in the tangle of grasses, brambles, wild flowers, weeds, nettles, briars and young saplings that cascaded down from the thick hedges that topped the gully's banks and bordered the narrow, twisting path at its floor. To Pat's unknowledgeable eyes it was a jungle to be negotiated with considerable care if his trousers were not to be torn by the intrusive brambles that bent menacingly down like barbed wire on a battlefront, or dirtied by thick clumps of tall vegetation in various stages of blossom and decay. His shoes, too, were under threat from the black ball-bearing-like droppings of rabbits that were spattered over the path itself.

He picked his way along, stepping delicately over the droppings, moving brambles by taking a leaf between finger and thumb and sliding past before releasing them, but it proved impossible to complete the journey unscathed. When the gully suddenly broadened out, and he found himself facing the wide rising expanse of the first of the Humps, a small tear and two brown smudges disfigured the storm-grey Gaultier slacks, several stitches hung loose from the burnt-orange sweater, smears of red on his hands illustrated the brambles' intractability, and the leather uppers of his hand-lasted shoes were smudged with dirty grey dollops of animal excrement.

Pat took out a handkerchief and wiped his hands. If this sort of journeying was necessary to get a glimpse of the warty newt it was hardly surprising that Ackers had seen at once that he was not a newt-lover. It was lucky in a way that Shelagh hadn't recognised him. If she had and he tried the newt stratagem she'd have seen through the pretence as quickly as Ackers had.

His clothes were the giveaway probably, but what did one wear in pursuit of the newt? There was probably some recognised uniform, like for hunting or shooting or fishing, though it seemed to him that a suit of armour would be best. Anyway, it was now clear that the success of his warty newt-hunter strategy depended on an adjustment of his wardrobe. A telephone call to his tailor would solve the problem, or maybe a trip to Stanton Proper would be quicker. As this was newt country they were bound to have something off the peg there. That was it. He'd do it first thing tomorrow.

Comforted by the decision Pat looked around. The trip through the gully had been arduous but despite it all he felt quite pleased with himself, and indeed dull would he have been of soul who, having fought his way through a perilous ditch, had not felt a twinge of pleasure at the sight that confronted him. Pat was a city lad, rich but with no landed background. A Londoner who had never been closer to a field than leaning on a gate.

Here the Humps rose up before him, great grassy mounds thick with buttercups. On one side hawthorn, hazel blackthorn and dogwood crowded the lower slopes.

The other was open to the sky providing an uninterrupted view of Longford Stanton, slightly different from the one at the other end of the gully, for the Rectory could be seen below the church tower and several other houses lined the edge of the village, their gardens and terraces clearly visible. It did not need a genius to see that they were there to take full advantage of the view. Development would ruin them.

A path zigzagged between the buttercups to the top of the first Hump. Pat climbed it steadily, resting now and then to take breath. The mound was not really very high, no more than a couple of hundred feet, but to him it was a mountain. By the time he reached the summit his legs were aching and he fell rather than sat down, regardless for once of any threat to his leisurewear.

Even before he recovered his breath he was blinking at what lay before him. It was like another country! He knew nothing of geology but plainly only something catastrophic in the past could have produced such contrasting landscapes in so small an area. The four Humps were grouped together in a rough diamond shape, their sides running smoothly down to form a deep basin below the level of the surrounding countryside. Between the Hump on which he stood and the next one, a smaller mound jutted into the basin. This he took to be the Pudden. Its attractions as a rendezvous for amatory dalliance were immediately obvious. It was bright with flowers, huge round bramble clumps, scattered bushes and tall grasses providing ample cover for lovers intent on enjoying the delights of alfresco sex. But beyond it the deep, uneven floor of the basin was covered almost completely with mossy growths and coarse heather-like plants, while here and there outcrops of rock, large and small, thrust themselves upwards as if endeavouring to escape the clutches of the surrounding vegetation.

It was hardly a place of beauty and Pat's first thought was that any newt living in that glum mess needed its head looked at. Using the basin as an infill wasn't a bad idea. Grass it over and it would end up fine and smooth like the Humps. He looked again at the Pudden and drew in an appreciative breath. A smooth grassy bank dotted with flowering clumps and bushes that offered privacy for all kinds of sexual frisking among the buttercups and daises. Alfresco sex – wow! A new experience! Fun beneath the sun as nature intended. He tingled at the thought, and set out to find, and mentally reserve, a suitable spot.

He was halfway down the path when, incredibly, Shelagh Breagh appeared from behind a huge bramble clump and stood looking down into the basin. It was unmistakably her. Pat stopped in his tracks. No more than five hundred yards separated them, but she had not seen him. Almost instinctively he stepped off the path and stood behind a hawthorn bush. It was necessary to give this piece of luck a little thought. Had she recognised him at the church a straightforward 'Hello, fancy meeting you here' would have established some kind of relationship, however tenuous. But one had to be careful with women!

It was important not to seem pushy or over-familiar. It might be best simply to exchange casual greetings, no more than a simple 'Good day' and a remark on the weather, before passing on one's way, leaving more effusive greetings for a call at the Rectory to arrange a visit to the Abbey ruins. She was bound to recognise him, then there would be apologies all round. A good start – if they met, of course.

There was no saying they would. The Rector might just shut the door and take him straight to the ruins. Pat clicked his teeth. What was he worried about? This was too good a chance to miss! There she was. Get to her – engage her in conversation – somehow excite her interest in him so that a future meeting could be arranged. Open up about the warty newt! Express interest but not expertise. The best way of getting attention was to ask advice. He would do that.

'I'm trying to find out more about the warty newt.'

'Really?'

'I've been reading this book – it says there are plenty up here.'

'There are.'

'Oh good. I just hope I can recognise one when I see it.'

'It's not difficult. Come on, I'll show you.'

As an introductory scenario it sounded faultless. His confidence rose. He looked round the bush and his confidence collapsed. Shelagh had been joined by a man! And they appeared to be behaving very affectionately towards each other.

Pat sucked in a breath of disbelief. It was like a shot from some romantic film – lovers together on a hill, silhouetted against the blue sky, a light breeze ruffling the girl's hair as they held hands, both hands, and looked into each other's eyes before coming together in a gentle, loving kiss. And Christ! That's just what they were doing! Kissing. Was it possible that...no, it couldn't be...yes, it could! Hard to get? Huh! She was female and she was with a male and females did not hold hands with males on hilltops and kiss them to make pretty pictures. Oh no! Kissing in such circumstances indicated that something had either already occurred behind the bramble clump or would very shortly. There could be no other explanation. It was what the Pudden was famous for, and the woman he was pursuing was honouring its tradition. Unfortunately she was not honouring it with him but with a man who looked, admittedly at a distance, as if he patronised a tailor who still believed that tweed was the 'in' thing, and flat caps *de rigueur* anywhere near a field. Shelagh, Pat noted, was wearing a pleated tartan skirt and what looked like a plum-coloured sweater. Nothing special, but knee deep in the grass as she lifted her face to be kissed she looked the epitome of femininity.

Pat felt a peculiar sensation in the region of his sternum, as if the light lunch he had enjoyed had compacted into a solid ball and lodged itself between his ribs. It was an unpleasant feeling. He swallowed hard, but the lump remained stubbornly in place.

The couple on the Pudden parted from their kissing position, let go each other's hands and stood for a second or so simply looking at each other. They exchanged a few words then the man turned and walked away. Shelagh watched him go, standing motionless until he reappeared after passing behind a bramble clump some distance away. She raised a hand and waved. In Pat Pendle's book it was not a wave of a last farewell to Cloth Cap as he walked into the sunset. Oh no! It was a see-you-next-Sunday, same-time-same-place-for-another-piece-of-pudding sort of wave. No doubt because it wouldn't do for the Rector's daughter to be seen coming from the Pudden with a man. The locals'd know what they'd been up to...and the locals'd be right.

The lump seemed to have stuck permanently between his ribs. It annoyed and irritated him; being moved or affected in any way by a woman's behaviour was a novel and not pleasing experience for Pat. Damn it all, what was the point of planning to deflower a woman who was not above rolling in the grass with some twit in tweeds and a flat cap! He might just as well pick up any stray village wench and... What's she up to now?

Across on the Pudden Shelagh had turned from watching Cloth Cap's departure and was stepping down towards the basin. It must have been a rather steep descent for she was out of sight almost immediately. Pat hesitated. His campaign had lost its savour, but if available to Cloth Cap she might just as easily be available to him. It would not be the delicious conquest he had imagined but he'd come a long way to tumble her – why leave without getting a taster of the alfresco scenario? It might be quite enjoyable, and at least some reward for an otherwise wasted journey – besides teaching her not to go round masquerading as Lady Innocent.

He ran down to the bottom of the Hump where the path joined another along the defile between the bases of the two mounds in the direction of the basin, making it unnecessary to climb the Pudden. A hundred yards or so along it began to slope steeply downwards, then abruptly he was on the edge of an even steeper incline, almost a cliff, and there, stretched below him like a neglected rockery in a huge crater, was the craggy wilderness of the Humps centre. There was no sign of Shelagh.

He walked around the edge which skirted the base of the Pudden to where a track sloped downwards to the floor of the basin. He followed it, now mossy and heather-lined, past rocky outcrops until it gradually petered out to nothing more than a faint marking in the bunched, close-packed heather. The ground was damp, bog-like; wet was beginning to seep through his shoes, he felt warm and clammy. Only when several large spots of rain spattered on his face did he notice that the sky had become overcast. Christ! It was going to bucket down! The thought had no sooner entered his head than the skies opened like sluice gates and a torrent of water flooded down to the earth.

Pat looked round desperately and ran to a large sloping outcrop of rock which offered some prospect of shelter. He reached it soaked almost to the skin, his storm-grey slacks clinging to his legs, his sweater dripping with water, his patterned socks squelching in the hand-crafted shoes.

The outcrop was like the slanting roof of a lean-to from which the supporting wall had been removed. Pat crouched hovering beneath it, beginning to curse the day he'd met the Rector's daughter. The sight of her had started him on what was intended to be a light-hearted sexual divertissement and here he was tucked under a bloody great lump of rock in the middle of nowhere, soaked to the skin, his beautiful, hand-lasted shoes ruined and more than likely catching his death of cold! He folded his arms across his chest and hunched his shoulders in an attempt to conserve some body heat and stop his shivering. The rain teemed down, pools of water beginning to form in the boggy ground outside, but fortunately beneath the outcrop it remained comparatively dry. Pat stamped his feet. If it got much worse a boat would be needed to rescue him, if he was still alive to be rescued! The way the rain was falling, and the pools linking up to form larger ones, the whole basin could end up a lake, flooding his shelter. He'd be found drowned – if great-horned newts left anything of him to be found! He silently cursed Shelagh Breagh.

"Are you all right?" said a female voice. He turned quickly, startled. The object of his imprecations was standing behind him.

"What! How...?" Pat struggled to find his voice. "Where did you come from?"

"You're absolutely soaked!"

"What the hell do you expect? It's pissing down! Can't you see?"

"There's no need for bad language."

"There is every bloody need," said Pat, irritated both by her calmness and the fact that she appeared to be completely dry. "And if you were as wet as I am you'd be using it too!"

"Why? Will it dry your clothes?"

"Don't try to be bloody funny! I could catch my death through this!" As if to confirm the possibility he gave vent to an explosive sneeze. "Christ! I knew it! This is going to kill me."

"You'd better come with me."

"Where?"

"If you come you'll see."

Virgin Victorious

Shelagh led her drenched and miserable prospective seducer deeper into the outcrop, through a cleft in the rock and along a tunnel that opened out into a large cavern, at one end of which a shaft of light could be seen, indicating another entrance. Two hissing portable gas lamps provided further illumination and were reflected in a stream of water that gushed along the lower end of the cavern's slightly sloping floor. Near the water were a camping stool, a haversack and what looked like a large notebook.

"What the hell place is this?"

"Some special newts breed here and I'm studying them for the environmental group I work with."

"You mean you sit in...aaaaa...tishooo!"

"I think you must get out of those wet things as quick as you can."

"I'd like to," said Pat heavily. "But perhaps you'll tell me what I can put on in their place – I didn't bring a change with me."

"Then you must take them off while I dry them."

"What?"

"I often light a fire here when it's cold." She indicated a heap of brushwood on one side of the tunnel through which they had entered the cavern. "Dead heather burns very well and it'll keep you warm while they're drying too."

Shelagh collected some of the brushwood, laid it on a pile of ashes, remnants of previous fires, and broke some of it into small pieces as tinder. Pat stared at her in wonderment, then gave vent to another huge sneeze.

"Aaaaa...tishooo!" It echoed round the cavern. "Atishooo!"

"Good heavens!" A match and the tinder flared. "It sounds as if you've really caught something. Get them off quickly and sit on this."

She fetched the camp stool from the waterside and placed it near the now crackling fire. "That should keep you warm. Now get them off."

Before Pat could protest she was lifting the hem of his sweater towards the head.

"If you bend down it'll be easier."

"I'll take them off myself," said Pat, feeling like a little boy being undressed for his bath. "If you don't mind!"

"I don't mind at all." She stepped back. "Only do get on with..."

She got no further. Pat let out another tremendous sneeze.

"You see," Shelagh continued when the echo had died down. "Every second you have them on makes it worse."

Pat removed his burnt-orange sweater as carefully as its condition allowed. While he unbuttoned his shirt she arranged the sweater on some sticks so that it caught the heat.

When he handed her his shirt she said, "This is very silly clothing to be tramping the Humps in – haven't you got anything better?"

"That sweater is Galderi," said Pat, stiffly, "and the shirt is from Benkerman's."

"That may be fashionable," the shirt joined the sweater on a stick, "but on the Humps it is wiser to be practical. The weather can be very changeable."

"I've found that out!"

"Then you'll know better next time. If you survive, of course!" She smiled sweetly. "Your trousers please."

Pat paused for a fractional moment. His image of her as the epitome of sexual diffidence was already tarnished by what he had just seen on the Pudden, but her tone was so matter-of-fact it seemed that asking men to remove their trousers was an every-day event with her.

"If you don't take them off you'll very likely get rheumatism or rheumatic fever or something."

He removed his shoes first – they were more black than brown from the soaking they'd received – and placed them a distance from the fire. As he turned from doing this he caught a glint of amusement in her eyes as she waited patiently, stick in hand, for his trousers.

"Shoes shouldn't be put near direct heat," he said defensively. "If they dry too quickly it ruins the leather. And these are handmade."

"Are your trousers handmade too?"

Pat hesitated only a moment. He kept himself in trim with sessions at Skidsy's gym – a good body was an asset to seduction. Why not let her see it?

"They're Gaultier," he said.

Unzipping the flies he stepped out of his trousers, keeping each leg clear of the cavern floor by a wobbly balancing act which entailed hopping from one foot to the other.

Shelagh laughed. He glared. She composed her face into an expression of mute gravity that did not succeed in quelling the laughter in her eyes, and held out her hand for the slacks.

He handed them to her, glad to be free of their clammy embrace, peeled off his socks and stood erect by the fire in his striped boxer shorts. They, too, were soaked, and clung tenaciously to his buttocks and crotch like a second skin. Their wet transparency revealing the dark shadow of his pubic hair and the moulded shape of his genitals beneath. He sat down hurriedly on the camp stool, arranging himself primly as a woman, his knees tight together.

"We'd better have those off," said Shelagh.

"What?"

"They're soaked as well, aren't they?" She pointed to his shorts. "Hardly surprising – your slacks are ridiculously thin!"

"They happen to be the latest style," said Pat stiffly.

"I'm sure they are. Now give the pants to me please. The sooner they're dry the better it'll be for you!"

"They can dry on me!"

"There's no need to be shy. We're both adults. I shan't get excited and attack or rape you or anything like that so take them off, come on."

"I'm not taking them off!"

"Aren't you being rather old-fashioned?"

Pat choked: he had romped naked round bedrooms with more women than he cared to remember, but they had been naked too. The idea of stripping himself before a fully clothed woman with no hope of reciprocation offended his masculine dignity. He was disadvantaged enough already without exposing himself completely to her amused scrutiny. A counter-attack was needed.

"I wouldn't want your boyfriend to arrive and get the wrong idea."

"What boyfriend?"

"Have you got a selection?" That was good! he thought. Barbed, sarcastic. Knock her matter-of-factness about a bit.

"Of course I have." Her matter-of-factness remained untouched. "I am not a recluse. I do not live in this cave. But supposing one did come in," she continued calmly, looking Pat straight in the eyes. She could play games too. "What sort of idea would he get?"

"Oh come on! Don't try the innocent – finding you with a naked man there's only thing he could think."

"And what exactly would that be?"

There was an amused glint in her eyes. Challenging him to be explicit. Well, all right, if that's how she wanted it she could have it!

"You know what fucking is, don't you?"

"Yes."

"Well, that's what he'd think we were doing. Fucking."

"Why? I'm not on my back and you're not on top of me."

The logic was indisputable, but it was the direct simplicity of the answer that dumbfounded Pat. He goggled at her.

She smiled back at him and, before he could collect his wits, continued, "You are wet and in a completely undesirable condition. Even a man could see that and, besides, I am fully clothed down to knickers and panties. It would require considerable imagination to sort out how intercourse was being effected." She smiled sweetly. "Don't you agree?"

"What?" said Pat stupidly.

His mind was refusing to function. All he could do was gawp unbelievingly, hypnotised by her casual, unembarrassed attitude.

"The truth is that you are shy – that's quite understandable but it would be better if you faced the truth rather than hide behind a spurious concern for my good name. I can't force you to remove your shorts but it would be wiser if you did. Now I must get on with some work. Keep the fire going."

Shelagh smiled again and went over to the pool where she busied herself with a net and peered into the water. Pat twisted round and stared at her. What kind of a bloody woman was she?! A wave of irritation engulfed him. She had humiliated him, treated him like a pimply youth who hadn't got past admiring himself in the mirror. Well he'd show her. He stood up abruptly, tore off his wet pants and slapped them on the floor of the cave with an almighty whack. Shelagh turned on the sound and he stood before her, naked, full frontal, hands on hips as if to say 'you wanted them and they're off. Now what? Who's old-fashioned and embarrassed now?'

"I'm glad you've seen sense," she said. "But don't leave them on the ground, they'll get dirty!"

Her offhandedness irritated him beyond endurance. He took a step forward and glared intimidatingly, determined to break her seemingly impregnable calm – certain that, confronted by a naked man in aggressive mood, she was bound to show some apprehension. He would then have the pleasure of dismissing her fear with a blast of withering sarcasm. It was already on the tip of his tongue – "Don't flatter yourself – I'd sooner have sex with one of your bloody newts!"

She gave him no chance, before he could open his mouth she said, "I saw everything you've got before you sat down. It's nothing special," and turned back to inspecting the pond.

It was only with a mighty effort of will that Pat resisted the impulse to grab his tormentor and shake her violently until she screamed for mercy. She had her back towards him, kneeling forward peering into the depths of the pool, her skirt lifted slightly, revealing the lower parts of her thighs. It was a vision that awakened erotic fantasies in Warwick Tewson during prayerful sessions in church, and it had no less an effect on Pat. He gazed, fascinated, at where the slightly parted thighs disappeared into the skirt towards the neatly rounded rump of Shelagh's bottom and experienced a jerky stiffening movement in the region of his crotch. He turned hurriedly away and sat by the fire, closing his legs. But this time his embarrassment rose above them.

CHAPTER FIVE

Oh Jesus – in his Pants

Warwick Tewson had the quakes. He spent the fifteen minutes or so of the drive to Stoke Kirby speculating on why Sir Archibald Pomfrey should invite them to tea at such short notice, and blaming Sylvia for accepting the invite. She knew, as he did, that he was not the caustic-tongued baronet's favourite MP. A summons to meet him usually involved severe condemnation of some aspect of government policy that did not meet his approval, accompanied by a demand that this be brought to the notice of the Minister of the department concerned.

In this instance Warwick's heightened state of nerves resulted from the terrifying thought that, while his own friends in Whitehall had kept him in the dark about the infill, Sir Archibald's might have been more forthcoming. It was true that Stoke Kirby would not be directly affected by whatever happened at the Humps but the baronet was a landed aristocrat of the old school and looked on the countryside surrounding his ancestral home as his personal fiefdom. There was also the possibility that the Pendle woman was in the know and had been blabbering.

Sylvia remained silent during her husband's mixture of complaint and conjecture, breaking it only to remark, when he told her for the tenth time that she should have said they were otherwise engaged, that as she was not a politician lying did not come naturally to her. Nor did she automatically see an invitation to tea as a summons to an Inquisition.

Although she did not admit it out loud, the invitation delighted her. Even had she known for certainty that it boded trouble for Warwick she would have accepted. Bridget Pendle would be at Stoke Kirby and the warm squeeze of her hand had awakened in Sylvia a new sense of being. She was hoping for more.

"And for God's sake," Warwick implored as they reached the Pomfrey mansion, "don't let on to anyone that we nearly had Pat Pendle as a guest this weekend – don't as much as mention his name. If his sister does, say you've never heard of him. Understand?"

"Any rubbish tip will not be your responsibility," Sylvia answered tartly. "Why not tell him that?"

As it turned out Warwick's fear appeared groundless. Sir Archibald greeted them cordially enough and during tea the conversation was devoted mainly to discussion of the Rector's sermon. Sir Archibald approved, and held forth on its merits at considerable length. The three women, Bridget, Paula and Sylvia remained quiet, exchanging smiles and only occasionally interjecting murmurs of agreement. Warwick felt vaguely uneasy, as if he were an unwelcome intruder on a conspiracy or secret society. As his host rambled on he found himself eyeing Bridget and Paula and wondering anew whether Pat's account of their relationship was believable. Warwick considered himself experienced and knowledgeable in the technique of sex from initial skirmishes to final ecstasy, but was baffled as to how two women could possibly approach each other with a view to doing whatever they did to each other. That it could be a relationship founded on love and requiring sexual expression as a consummation was beyond his understanding. What preoccupied his mind was how they went about the business of seduction. It was difficult to imagine two women kissing and cuddling and exciting each other to the point where they hopped into bed and got down to the real business. As far as he could see, one of them at least was going to be disappointed!

"It's like the damned government, eh Tewson!" Sir Archibald's barking articulation broke into his thoughts. "Can't trust a thing they say."

"I beg your pardon."

"The weatherman! Promised sunshine and look what we've got!"

Outside the window the rain had started to fall in torrents. Gusts of wind lashed it against the panes.

"Can't blame the government for that," said Warwick smugly.

"It's a fair reflection of how the country is, and we know who's to blame for that!" Sir Archibald got to his feet. "We'll leave the ladies to their gossip. I want to speak to you privately."

Warwick's stomach, which had settled down somewhat, returned to the *status quo* ante. Bridget flashed him a sympathetic smile which did nothing to reassure him. She probably knew what the 'private talk' was about.

The study was furnished with a desk, several bookshelves, a number of busts of previous Pomfreys, an orrery and two leather armchairs. After seating his guest in one of these, Sir Archibald stood leaning back against the desk for what, to Warwick, seemed long minutes before speaking.

"So you're selling your house," he said flatly.

"It's really too large for us and..."

"The reasons don't matter. You're selling it?"

"Yes. You see..."

"How about buying this one? You'll need a replacement, won't you?"

Warwick stared at the baronet. "Eh?" he said stupidly.

"I want to sell it quickly and get out of the damned country. Can't stand it any more. Not while you and the rest of the crew we've got as a government is in office. So what about it? Are you interested in buying it or not? You'll save a bit if you do; none of those blood-sucking agents after their cut so I'll let it go at a reasonable price. What d'you say?"

"I...er..." said Warwick weakly, so taken aback by the news and comment that he found difficulty in collecting his wits. "I...er...I don't understand – you're selling because of the government...er..."

"Can't call it a government – pushing the interest rate up and down and lying in their teeth when driven to earth... Can't call that governing! Look at you – nothing personal, but only interested in your own skin, aren't you?"

It was, Warwick had to admit, one aspect of his character, but not one for public display to his constituents, and certainly not to an old aristocrat whose ideas about public service and *noblesse oblige* were politically inconvenient.

"It's a government you support, Sir Archibald," he said defensively. "And if I..."

"Support! Where'd you get that idea? No gentleman could support this government. They're traders, everyone one of them. They call themselves businessmen but traders are what they are and they've got traders' values! If there's one thing we aristocrats have been right about all along it's to distrust traders – we've always looked down on them, so have the workers, and it's God's pity we never got together to get rid of 'em. They only see what's rung up on the till and there's nothing they won't sell if there's a profit to be made. It's made this country no place for a gentleman."

"What we are doing", said Warwick, struggling for a suitable cliché from the party's policy statements, "is to make the country more efficient."

"Efficiency," barked Sir Archibald, "for traders is profit; it has nothing to do with making people happy. It is the death of humanity. Damn me if Marx wasn't right about the bourgeoisie and damn me if I ever thought I'd say that... Now what about the house? It's here in your constituency, couldn't be more suitable and I'll let you have it at valuation – what d'you say?"

"But it's your ancestral home. Surely..."

"No one to leave it to. No sons, and Paula tells me she's no intention of having children, so what's the point? Why suffer in this God-forsaken country? May as well sell up, get away from the filth, hypocrisy, violence and general money-grabbing and live somewhere civilised... So what do you say?"

Warwick found it difficult to believe his ears – his luck! Stoke Kirby was in poor repair, but it was a fine old house, Jacobean in parts, and properly restored could prove a profitable investment. But the overwhelming blessing – the real bunce – was it put him in the clear, gave him a cast-iron defence against any accusations of inside knowledge or opportunism that might arise when the news of the infill became known. All he had to do was claim he was selling his own house to buy Sir Archibald's! And with the baronet in Italy or somewhere, there was no one to prove it had been otherwise. It was almost too good to be true! He was being handed escape on a platter.

"Well?" demanded Sir Archibald.

"I'm flattered, naturally," said Warwick cautiously, "and interested, yes, but may I ask why I'm being favoured with the...the...er...offer?"

"If I put it on the open market some damn speculator will get hold of it and fill the grounds with semi-detached rabbit hutches. I think I can trust you not to do that – not if you want to get re-elected."

Sir Archibald opened a bookcase and took out a bottle of whisky and two glasses. Warwick ruminated. The old boy had it weighed up, but that was a short-term outlook. In the long term – well, in the long term the day would come when he'd be finished with politics, and when it did the constituency party could go hang!

"There's also the fact that I know Sylvia likes the place and wouldn't allow you to desecrate it – she's always said she'd like to live here." Sir Archibald handed Warwick a whisky and faced him with one in his own hand. "Is it a deal?"

"Subject to price," said Warwick.

"Subject to price," said Sir Archibald and raised his glass. "It's a deal then?"

"It's a deal," said Warwick, and raised his own.

On the way back to Longford Stanton Warwick told Sylvia about his conversation with Sir Archibald.

"Oh good," she said placidly. "You'll like living at Stoke Kirby."

"Won't you?"

"I've always been fond of it."

"It solves all our problems. If the price is right, of course."

"Of course."

They drove for a while in silence, Sylvia smiling to herself.

"What did you talk about with Paula and the Pendle woman?"

"Oh...this and that," she said.

Ackers the Comforter

The bar of the Beak and Wedge was empty when Pat

Pendle entered to restore his battered ego with as large a whisky as could be reasonably ordered without actually asking for the bottle. His trek back from the Humps had been every bit as humiliating as his experience in the cave. As soon as his clothes were dry he had left Shelagh to the warty newts, glad to escape her total indifference to his presence and nakedness. Unfortunately his hand-crafted shoes proved their unsuitability for hiking by disintegrating so completely that by the time he reached the gully they had separated into their constituent parts. The stitching appeared to have rotted through.

He was cursing his luck, damning the makers to perdition and wondering how he could possibly negotiate the gully in his socks when Ackers had appeared as if from nowhere and volunteered to carry him piggy-back to the Inn. Having little alternative he had reluctantly accepted, only to be overtaken by Shelagh at the end of the gully. She had exchanged a cheery greeting with Ackers, totally ignored Pat and turned off up the lane to the Rectory.

Consuming his whisky Pat seethed at the indignity of it all. A hot bath had soothed his body somewhat but the hurt to his self-esteem tormented more with every passing minute. He wanted revenge. He wanted to get his hands on Shelagh Breagh and teach her that he was not a man to be slighted.

He wanted to teach her till she cried for mercy, but he couldn't fathom how to get her into a position for the kind of teaching he had in mind. To seduce a woman it is essential to achieve some kind of relationship, however tenuous, that will induce in her a willingness to accept bodily contact. How could one do that with a woman who hardly bothered to acknowledge your existence even when you were naked before her? Sorting that out was going to require some serious drinking.

"Old Armpits was asking after you," said the porter–

barman as he refilled the glass. "Wanted to know what you were doing here."

Pat ruminated. "Armpits, oh yes, the barrel of lard in tweeds?"

"That's him, sir. Oh dearie me. Yes. Barrel of lard! You've met him then?"

Pat took a drink. He was not going to get involved in trying to explain the encounter in the toilet.

"Only he seemed very interested in you, sir."

"Oh did he?"

"Seemed to think you were a friend of Mr Ackers."

"I am a friend to Mr Ackers. He's been a great help to me."

"Mr Pitts had a special sort of friend in mind, if you know what I mean, sir."

Pat very definitely did, but he sensed the barman–porter was using the incident to try to discover why he was in the village. Much as Ackers had been doing. He decided to counter-attack.

"Are you always so curious about who comes here?"

"Only them as is different, sir," said the porter. "Ordinaries we don't bother about."

"How do you know who's not ordinary?"

"No trouble, sir, oh dearie me no! Tell them a mile off. Developers particular. Developers aren't liked round here."

"Do you think I'm a developer?"

"No saying what you could be, sir. That's the trouble. Round here we don't like not knowing. There's trouble in not knowing. But now I know you're Mr Ackers' friend...oh, and fancy that, sir. Here he is. You'll be buying him a pint, I expect."

Ackers accepted the pint with gratitude. Pat took him away from the bar to a table in the corner. Ackers was not surprised to hear that Pitts had been giving tongue.

"You stung him. It's his way of getting his own back."

"Hrrump!"

"What's the worry to you – won't be staying here will you? Not now you've had an eyeful of the newts."

"What were you doing on the Humps?"

"Lucky for you, wasn't it?"

"Yes – but what were you doing there?"

"Watching you, o'course," said Ackers cheerfully. "You're up to something and I'm nosy by nature."

"You mean you followed me?"

Ackers nodded, grinned and buried his face in his beer. Pat felt himself go pink round ears.

"How far did you follow me?"

"I had to keep dry, didn't I?"

Pat went to the bar for another refill to cover his confusion. When he returned Ackers was carefully rolling a cigarette.

"If you'd followed me you'd have been as wet as I was. And I'd have seen you."

"I got my ways," said Ackers. "Didn't ask her much about newts, did you?"

Pat took a deep drink from his refilled glass. The situation was getting out of hand. It was bad enough being humiliated by a woman but to know that there'd been a witness... He half-choked on his drink. If the story ever got back to London he'd be a laughing stock.

"You don't have to worry about me," said Ackers shrewdly. "I don't talk out of turn."

His perception irritated Pat. "What's the idea? Why are you following me around? I'm not a bloody celebrity."

"Famous firm, yourn," said Ackers. "Pendle's Disposal. I'm told it's the biggest in its line. You must be a millionaire."

"Do you want my autograph or my notecase?"

Ackers chuckled. "I'm just interested why a

millionaire muckspreader goes clambering over the Humps claiming he's a newt-watcher." He eyed Pat steadily. "You got any ideas of doing business hereabouts? And I don't mean newt-collecting."

"I'm getting sick of this," said Pat peevishly. "What the hell has it got to do with you or anyone else why I'm here? And I don't like being cross-examined. You stick to your thieving. I'll mind my business. That way we'll all be happier."

"Now, now, now!" said Ackers placidly. "No need to get short-tailed round your shirt front. All I'm telling you is if there's anything you want to know about the Humps, I'm your man. Nothing I don't know."

"I don't give a damn about the Humps. But if you are so knowledgeable you can tell me – just out of curiosity – who was that tweedy twit the Rector's daughter was kissing on the Pudden?"

"That's her ex-intended. Name of Hawkins."

"Ex?"

"That's it. They were engaged, now it's off."

"It didn't look very off to me."

"Well, it is...and Miss Breagh's not one for changing her mind. With her, off'll be off."

"Huh," said Pat.

"Tell you what," said Ackers, eyeing him quizzically. "I'll get you another drink." He got up and went to the bar.

Pat sat moodily, images of Shelagh in the cave flitting through his mind's eye like frames from an old movie. Damn it all. There was something fascinating about her. It wasn't just that she had a magnificent figure and a face like an angel...angel! What was he thinking of! She had treated him like...like a...

Before he could reach a conclusion as to just what she was like, Ackers returned and placed a whisky before him.

"Cheers," said Ackers, lifting his refilled pot.

"Cheers," said Pat, still searching for a simile to describe the humiliation he had suffered.

"That was a funny do about Miss Breagh," said Ackers carefully. "How she treated you. What I mean is," he continued pointedly, as Pat eyed him with baleful suspicion, "women don't ignore men like that without there's something they're after – it's usually a sort of calculated come-on, eh?"

Three treble whiskies and a double had partly assuaged the pain of Pat's wounded pride by inducing a mood of self-pity, and fuddling his mental faculties. So it was a second or two before the full significance of Ackers's remark registered in his brain. When it did it hit with the full force of Saul's revelation on the way to Damascus. The cloud of unknowing dispersed and he was enveloped in the bright sun of true knowledge.

He could have embraced Ackers. 'It's usually a calculated come-on!' Of course! That is exactly what it was. She was deliberately ignoring him to make him more interested in her. She knew she had him on a hook and was playing him like a fish... Right – well, he knew a trick or two like that himself. Never mind the newts and alfresco dalliance – this was a clear case of softly softly up the garden path to where honesty was truly the best hypocrisy. Sincerity the key.

"You feeling all right?"

"What?"

"You look like you've had a hot flush," said Ackers.

Oh Jesus Triumphant

Along Whitehall the traffic was jammed to a standstill. Simultaneous light failures in Trafalgar Square and Parliament Square had imprisoned a hooting mass of frustrated humanity in their status symbols. Pedestrians coughed and wheezed their way through the poisonous, lead-laden haze that even the drizzle of fine rain could not disperse. It was the sort of day that fills travel agents' offices with eager emigrants and puts the Samaritans on full alert. Nevertheless even the sun-drenched glamour spots of the world could not have produced a lighter step than Warwick Tewson's as he blithely made his way on foot from the House to the office of the Ministry of Rural Affairs.

It was not just that the Prime Minister had smiled at him, though this undoubtedly counted as a plus to the day, or that he had fended off his Shadow's query on pig-slurry pollution with a brisk, "It is not the policy of the government to comment on any subject within the purview of the Animal Waste Products Disposal and Retrieval Standing Committee which is sitting to consider the possibility of a review of its remit within the broader scope of powers embodied in the recent Land Use Bill currently being debated in another place."

He made a mental note to ask Porson what it meant, but what really occupied his mind and lightened his step was the news that a price had been agreed for the purchase of Stoke Kirby and an offer made for his own house, Marble Lodge. He had instructed his solicitor, Benjamin Brewer of Brewer, Brewer, Innis and Brewer, to clinch both deals with all speed. Not only that, but discreet enquiries of Legget at the Supply had elicited the fact that the unloading of whatever was to be unloaded at the Pollocks would not be arriving until well after the House rose for Summer Recess. This provided a lapse of several months between his moving house and the start of the infill. It also neatly sidestepped the possibility of any immediate loaded questions from the Opposition. Not that he feared that now. He was in the clear. It had all been sorted out very nicely. Rain was falling on Whitehall but the sun was shining on Warwick Tewson.

Tea for Two-gether

In so far as the Pendle family could be said to have a tradition it was the partaking of tea on Friday nights. How the tradition came to be established no one quite knew, but it was tacitly assumed that on that day each week the three children attended their parents' house in old Camberwell for tea and cake. Tim (Bridget's twin) believed it had its origins in Mrs Pendle's shopping habits. In their younger days, when the family fortunes were an unrealised dream, Friday was the day their mother laid in supplies for the weekends. These invariably included a cake as a treat for her brood when they returned from school, and they came to look upon it as a sort of celebration to welcome their release from the rigours of education for the next two days.

Time and fortune had taken them from the parental home but, on leaving, each had promised to see Mum for tea on Fridays. Thus the habit had become ingrained and, other commitments permitting, the five Pendles assembled each Friday for tea and cake to gossip and exchange news, Mrs Pendle presiding. On this particular Friday Bridget was absent.

"She's staying with a friend somewhere," said Mrs Pendle, wielding her silver teapot, "and rang me on the telephone to say she couldn't come."

"She's with Paula Pomfrey, I think," said Tim to Pat.

Tim was tall and slim, resembling his twin only in his colouring and deep eyes. His manner was gentle, relaxed, conveying a sense of inner peace, whereas Bridget was outgoing – magnetic. It was a source of wonderment to Pat that such different persons could have shared the same womb.

"You knew her, didn't you, son?" said Mr Pendle.

"Yes I did."

"He introduced her to Bridget," said Tim, and smiled

at Pat as if sharing a mildly humorous joke, "who is excessively fond of the aristocracy."

"Oh, nobs, are they?"

"Very – a baronetcy dating back to the Norman Conquest, but there's no son so where the title will go nobody knows."

"You should have married her," said Mrs Pendle to Pat, "then maybe you'd have got it."

"It doesn't work out like that, Mum."

"I'd like to have been a lord," said Mr Pendle biting deeply into a large slice of Black Forest gateau.

"Oh you don't mean that, Dad!" Mrs Pendle sounded almost scandalised and sat upright in her chair, the silver teapot in her hand seeming to share her astonishment at such a confession.

"I do. Then I could wear all that gear they get dressed up in. Lovely, all red and white and that thing on my head."

"You'd look silly."

"So what? There'd be a lot of others looking silly with me!"

Pat exchanged an amused look with Tim. "Make a large enough donation to the party in power," he said, "and I dare say you'd get one!"

"You kiddin'?"

"I don't know quite how it's done but it has been done."

"Um," said Mr Pendle.

"Waste of money," said his wife.

After tea Mr Pendle left for the local Boys' Club, in which he took a benevolent interest. Mrs Pendle hurried to the front room to watch a soap opera that had her enthralled.

Tim said to Pat, "I haven't seen you around town."

"I've been in the country."

"Oh!" Tim raised an eyebrow. "Are you going green?"

"I am chasing a bit of greenery."

"Tch, tch! You are incorrigible, Pat. You should marry and settle down."

"You can talk!"

"I am settled – Tony and I are perfectly happy together. Unfortunately I can't explain it to Mother, and as for Bridget... Is she serious with Paula?"

"As far as she's ever likely to be with anyone."

"Then you are Mother's only hope. You should take the plunge for her sake. She's longing for grandchildren and I must say I'm quite attracted to the idea of being an uncle."

"I'd be happy to oblige you both," said Pat, "if children came ready-wrapped without a woman in tow."

CHAPTER SIX

Passion Reconsidered

Driving back to Longford Stanton Pat tried to assess realistically his chances with Shelagh. After his talk with Ackers he had returned to London thinking it best to avoid any chance meeting in the village, and in the hope that time and absence might do a bit of defrosting. To help the process along he had then sent her a dozen red roses with a brief note apologising for the embarrassment he must have caused.

To prevent her rejecting the apology, or thanking him for it, he had been careful to put no address on the note. His intention now was to contrive to meet her 'accidentally' in Longford Stanton when, he reasoned, she was bound to say something and, kind or caustic, he intended to respond with shy humility, a tactic he believed capable of softening the hardest female heart. Her forgiveness obtained, his next move would be to invite her to dinner, suggesting in the same shy, diffident manner that only then would he feel he had been truly shriven. Having thus breached the wall of indifference he was confident of his ability to undermine the resistance of the citadel itself and obtain surrender. He was conscious, however, that if this ploy failed it was difficult to see how he could proceed further without committing himself to a long-term strategy, which would involve wheedling himself into the social life of Longford Stanton – if there was any – so that he could meet her casually and rely on time and propinquity to establish a relationship. Any other approach, if the current one failed, could only be counter-productive. Women did not take men to their beds to rid themselves of an over-attentive nuisance.

The porter at the Beak and Wedge greeted him like an old friend. "And there's a letter for you, sir. It's got 'To Await Arrival' on it. So someone's expecting you. Oh yes, dearie me."

Pat's heart missed a beat but it was a false alarm.

"Mr Bickles's young lady dropped it in," continued the porter as he handed over a buff envelope. "Thinking of settling down here are you, sir?"

He hovered while Pat read the letter. Messrs Bickles, Estate Agents and Surveyors, thanked him for the favour of his instructions and were happy to inform him that they had a suitable property available for a short rent. If he would be kind enough to call during office hours arrangements could be made for him to inspect it.

He tucked the letter in his pocket, told the porter to take care of his bags and went immediately to see Mr Bickles, whose office was situated in the cobbled area adjacent to the bookshop. As he turned the corner he came face to face with Shelagh.

It was a petrifying moment of mutual shock! They stood stock still and stared at each other. There was no question of her not recognising him this time, and he was gratified to see a faint blush redden her cheeks.

After what seemed an eternity she said, "Hello."

"Hello," said Pat awkwardly, totally unprepared to exploit the situation as he had envisaged it.

"Thank you for the roses – and the apology."

"Er...not...not at all."

"There was really no need, but thank you all the same."

For a moment she seemed to hesitate as Pat fought to

find words. Then she walked past him, and by the time he had recovered enough to turn in a desperate attempt to re-establish contact she had disappeared round the corner, any chance of getting his plan into gear disappearing with her.

Pursuit Renewed

The arrival of the roses at the Rectory had sent Mrs Breagh into a paroxysm of curiosity and hope. The Rector contented himself with a raised eyebrow, remarked that even love did not excuse extravagance, and retired to his study to compose a sermon on lust. His wife let fly a barrage of questions, convinced that the flowers were a peace offering from Andrew. Shelagh gave nothing away and went to her room, leaving her mother to start another search for the lost ring.

Since her adventure with Pat Pendle on the Humps Shelagh had experienced some pangs of remorse, feeling that her treatment of him might have been too harsh, cruel even. Her concern for his health when he was soaked and sneezing had been perfectly genuine. It was his tragi-comic dignity that had awakened in her the imp of teasing mischief that culminated in his full-frontal challenge to her modesty; and her cool dismissal of that had been nothing more than a desperate effort to keep a straight face and stop herself laughing. It had been the same when she came across him being carried piggyback by Ackers. If she had not passed quickly she would have been unable to stop herself laughing out loud, which would have humiliated him more.

All this would doubtless have delighted Maggie Williams but, by the time she reached the Rectory, Shelagh's amusement had evaporated. A new and surprisingly disturbing thought had occurred to her. What if she had so humiliated Pat that he abandoned his pursuit of her and returned to London?

The possibility that she had gone too far nagged at her mind so much that she made a discreet enquiry at the Beak and Wedge, only to have her fears confirmed. Mr Pendle had left.

The news plunged her into deep gloom, and she was considering – not by any means for the first time – devoting her life to good works when the roses arrived. Her gloom lifted, but only partially. The lack of an address on the card could be interpreted as a final 'brush-off'. Sort of saying I'm a gentleman even if you're not a lady. On the other hand some sixth sense warned her that it was, or might be, the opening shot in a softening-up process.

She was still debating the possible motives behind the roses when she bumped into Pat outside the estate agents. His obvious embarrassment had embarrassed her and, hardly knowing what she was doing, she had made her own apology and escaped – her heart thumping.

It would be interesting to see his next move, but she was now certain she was right. He had not given up the chase! Meanwhile she had her leaflets to deliver. Sir Archibald wanted the Humps to be declared a Site Of Special Scientific Interest, a sentiment she wholeheartedly agreed with, though why he'd called a meeting about it at such short notice was a bit of a mystery.

"Back again, eh? Well! I can't believe the newts is the attraction!" Ackers dropped into the seat opposite Pat in the bar of the Beak and Wedge, clutching a pint pot in his hand. "Newts don't need furnished houses, do they?"

"Is there anything your nose doesn't get into?"

"Not a lot," said Ackers.

Pat sipped his beer. He was in no mood for a question-and-answer session. It seemed to him that fate or some gremlin was putting the boot in his attempts to seduce Shelagh Breagh. To make matters worse she had looked more damnably attractive than ever when the red of embarrassed surprise had coloured her cheeks, and something had happened to the pit of his stomach that had nothing to do with wanting to get into bed with her. This was a completely new experience for him.

Alarm bells were beginning to tinkle in his subconscious, some sixth sense was warning him of a trap. The bait was beautiful, eminently desirable, but to enjoy that tempting morsel of femininity one had to risk the possibility that one might be unable to let go. Not because she was deliberately concealing a hook – no, he didn't think that, not now! Not after that blush. Her behaviour in the cave certainly baffled him, but he felt somehow that that blush defeated Ackers' analysis. She had not been giving him the come-on. No! She was unspoiled, and the hook he feared was that she promised the sort of delight that was addictive, making it impossible to countenance sharing her with anyone else. In short he had seen the pram in the hall!

Outside the estate agents he had dithered. Torn between the instinct to run for safety and reluctance to abandon the chase. Instinct lost. He took the house for a month, reasoning with the plausible sophistry of lust that he was letting his imagination run wild. It was ridiculous even to entertain the idea that he would get enamoured of some country mouse of a Rector's daughter. He would win her, enjoy her, and that would be that – another female scalp to add to an already impressive total. But there was no chance of seducing her in a room in the local Inn. He needed somewhere private, and the little cottage Messrs Bickles had on offer was ideal. Cosy, rose-bowered and tucked away near the edge of the village.

"What I wanted to tell you," said Ackers, "is Vi'll look after you. You'll be all right with her."

"Vi? Who's Vi?"

"My missus – they told you she goes to the cottage didn't they?"

"They said there was a woman..."

"That's Vi."

"Good grief!"

"I know the feeling," said Ackers sympathetically. "But her heart's in the right place and she can't help being disappointed how things are. Anybody'd be, wouldn't they?"

"I don't know what the hell you're talking about!"

"She's middle-aged and married – naturally she was born too late to be liberated – well, that's disappointing for a woman. Trouble is, she blames me for it – as if I was liberated, knew all along she wasn't, and denied it her. Like I should have been a Christian before Jesus Christ came along and told us we ought to be." Ackers shrugged his shoulders, defensive for the first time since Pat had met him. "I don't see why I should carry the can for history. I didn't make it and there's nothing I can do to change it. I mean, if she wants to go I'm not stopping her; if she wants to stay, I'm not saying no to that either. I'm not standing in her way. Oh no! There's nothing I make her do for me. If she don't want to wash or cook or whatever, all right I tell her. I'll manage, I'll do me own so she can be free. Do you think she's happy? Not on your life she's not. I'm selling her short, taking the mickey. What I'm doing, you see – and I'm telling as you're still a young man – is paying the penalty of falling in love with ideas we both believed in when we were young, and pledging we knew not what, cos that's how it was then. Now things have changed and I've to carry the can... Like it's my fault she was born female. Sex is all a matter of class... No, it is! Men like me don't have the power to free women; we can't even free ourselves. Women don't see that. We're prisoners, and I don't need to tell you who the gaolers are, do I?"

"Don't tell me to..." Pat began but the words dried in his mouth and he stared fixedly past Ackers's head as if he had seen a mirage. Ackers twisted in his seat. There was nothing there to excite interest, so he twisted back. Pat had recovered and was getting up.

"What's up?" said Ackers.

"Mind your own business," snapped Pat.

He bolted across the bar and out through the glass doors to the reception lounge. He had not been mistaken. There, talking to the receptionist, was Shelagh!

He stopped just inside the lounge and steadied himself. This time there was going to be no mistake. The ice had been broken – a shy diffidence, properly presented, ought to melt it completely, but whatever happened he must coax her into more than an abrupt exchange and flight. She was arranging something with the receptionist, handing her a leaflet from a packet. Probably a list of church services...that might be a good opener...but best not interrupt...wait...catch her on the turn as you...as you are...

'I was just collecting my key...'

No dammit, that was inviting her to say she wouldn't detain him...

'Good Lord! Fancy meeting you here...'

Banal! Pat fingered his tie. He wished he was wearing a coat instead of the striped Gigallian blouson – he had an idea she preferred formal dressing...and slacks are a bit...oh God, she'd finished. She's turned around. She's looking straight at me. She's going out...say something!

"Er," said Pat, the shy diffidence manifesting itself as pure adolescent gaucherie. She gave him a dazzling smile. His knees crumbled and he grasped a nearby chair for support.

"Are you feeling all right?"

"Oh yes...yes..." Pat found his voice with difficulty. "I was just...er... This is a surprise."

"We do seem to be running into each other... You staying here?"

"I am. Yes."

She stepped closer to him. His stomach somersaulted and went in search of his knees.

"Business or just a holiday?"

"I...er...holiday. Well, I...er...I'm having a sort of break. Get away from the City. I...er...cities get you down... I like to get...out...out into the country." He gabbled on, desperate to regain some sort of equilibrium and advance his cause. "Walk a bit...get some air. I...er...well...you live here of course."

"My father's the Rector."

"The Rector! Well...that's lovely. I mean – you know the district very well then?"

"I've lived here most of my life. If there's anything you'd like to know about it – where to visit, what to see – I'd be happy to help you."

Pat found it difficult to believe his ears. He'd been fighting for an opening and she was presenting it to him on a plate.

"That's very kind...yes...there are...I'd...er...perhaps you'd like to have dinner with me...and I...I...er..." He stumbled to a halt and mentally kicked himself. What the hell had got into him? She was only a woman; when had women ever been difficult to talk to? Yet here he was blabbing away like tongued-tied teenager. Oh God, he'd moved too fast. She'll back off. But she didn't! At least not exactly.

"That would be nice," she said. "But I don't eat in restaurants."

"You don't!?"

"I don't trust the food. One never knows where it comes from or what they've done to it. At home or in a private house with friends at least one can be sure it's clean and properly cooked, if nothing else."

"Well, we needn't eat here. I have a house...I've rented a house. We could eat there...I...er...I'm not a bad cook."

"That sounds lovely. When?"

"T-t-tomorrow?"

"That sounds very nice."

"We could meet here. Say seven?"

"Good, why not." She flashed him another of her knee-weakening smiles. "I'll look forward to it. Goodbye till then."

Shelagh walked briskly through the Inn door. Pat stood in a daze, hardly able to believe his luck. He had anticipated a difficult, subtle campaign, yet here she was, falling into his hands like a ripe apple. All that about not eating in restaurants...it was as good as asking for it. Almost as if she was saying, here I am, all ready to be plucked...and by God, thought Pat, am I going to enjoy the plucking!

He turned back the bar for a celebratory drink. Ackers was by the glass doors.

"I'll tell the missus to get in early," he said. "I dare say you'll want the place tidied – and the bed aired."

Virgin Unsure

Shelagh wondered if she had been too hasty – too forward. Maybe too ready an acceptance of his invitation made it look as if she was...well, available. She would have to be careful... Careful? Good heavens, careful of what? Pat Pendle might have reputation, a way with women but he was hardly likely to... No, no of course he wasn't...and she could handle him...well she had on the Humps and...and then she remembered the meeting about them Sir Archibald had called. If she dined with Pat Pendle she'd miss it... Ah well, no one was keener for the Humps to be kept unspoiled than she was...her job was more or less dedicated to it but...she could ring up Pat and explain...put off the date. Conservation was important, very important...yes, but so were other things and really she didn't...hmmmmm...it was a conundrum...he'd probably gone shopping for the meal...it wouldn't really be fair to...and Sir Archibald had rather sprung it on her...

Triumph Turns Sour for Oh Jesus

The Minister of Rural Affairs arrived home for the weekend relaxed, feeling that as far as things could be well in the world that was what they were. There would be a slight delay in completion of the house sale and purchase but, with the late starting date for the infill, that was no bother.

He had been unable to contact Pat Pendle – not that he mattered much now. Things looked like running smoothly enough without his cooperation. It was all very snug and satisfying – particularly the knowledge that Stoke Kirby's investment potential promised to yield a huge and profitable return – when he retired. He began to feel almost grateful to the Cabinet for keeping him in the dark – had he known what was planned he would have protested and tried to stop it...and been much the poorer had he succeeded!

Sylvia was wheeling a tea trolley from the kitchen when he arrived. He greeted her affectionately and even the news that Paula Pomfrey and Bridget Pendle were on the terrace did not entirely dampen his good spirits.

"They've been taking a really good look over the house," said Sylvia. "To see how they'll organise things."

"We're not going to be stuck with another charity do, are we?"

"Of course not! Furniture, curtains...who'll have which bedroom – that sort of thing."

"Who'll have whi... Should I know what you're talking

about?"

"They're buying the house – surely you know that!"

If the PM had appeared and offered to resign in his favour Warwick could not have been more stunned. His mouth opened and shut noiselessly.

"Didn't Bickles tell you?" asked Sylvia.

Warwick found his voice. "I didn't speak to Bickles. I spoke to Brewer."

"Didn't he tell you?"

"Would I be standing here poleaxed if he had?"

"And you didn't ask?"

"Oh Jesus!" Warwick's favourite expletive burst from him like a pricked balloon. "All I wanted was a buyer for the bloody place. I wasn't bothered who it was!"

"Then why are you making such a fuss?"

"Oh Jesus!" This time it was more an appeal than an expletive. "How am I going to get out of this one?" He walked about the hall, resisting the temptation to bang his head on the wall.

"Out of what one?"

"Don't cross-question me!"

"Are you coming in to tea?"

"Go and stuff them with cake. I've got to think this out!"

Sylvia shrugged and went off to entertain her guests. Warwick retired to his study, poured himself a stiff whisky and sat gloomily in an armchair.

The news had so stunned him that he found it difficult to sort out exactly what its implications were. Sir Archibald was a power in the party, and not only locally. He had the ear of the people in power even if he was dissatisfied with the way they operated. When the news of the infill broke, the Freedom of Information Act wouldn't stop him berating Warwick personally – and it would be no use pleading ignorance. Sir Archibald would know why he'd put his house on the market.

Warwick was also only too aware that he owed his seat to Sir Archibald's influence in the constituency – an influence secured by the latter's devotion to the memory of his old friend, Sylvia's father. The question was, would that devotion overcome Sir Archibald's wrath when he discovered that his daughter had been sold a pup? It certainly would not! The Pomfreys were slow to anger, but once roused – ugh! Warwick shivered. Of course Sir Archibald would probably be living abroad by the time the news broke. On the other hand he might not! Warwick shivered again. It would make no difference anyway – oceans would not shield him from the Pomfrey's vengeance. He could wave ta-ta to the Longford Stanton seat – the local party would disown him. As for his prospect of a title...forget it!

Warwick poured himself another drink. A thought occurred. The next most powerful man in the local party was Rigger...Tommy Rigger. With Sir Archibald away he would undoubtedly take control and, importantly, Rigger was a developer on a large scale. He had opposed Pitts' piddling little development – it would have made him unpopular in the party – Stoke Kirby was a different proposition.

Warwick's gloom began to lift a little. Rigger was no sentimentalist; he had none of Sir Archibald's scruples. Horse-trading was second nature to him. He understood quid pro quos and the offer of a partnership in the future development of Stoke Kirby would promise him enough quids to secure the important quo of his support for Warwick's continuance as Member for the Longford Stanton constituency.

Heartened by his reasoning Warwick's upbeat mood began to reassert itself. Deciding that he could not completely ignore his wife's guests he made his way to the terrace. Then he remembered that one of them was Pat Pendle's sister – and felt a quake of alarm. Second thoughts reassured him. Sylvia had said Paula Pomfrey and the Pendle were buying the house jointly, which clearly proved that both were ignorant of the coming infill. This amused Warwick. Two leses setting up house and one a member of the family being paid to ruin the house's value. Talk about being hoist with your own whatnot! That'd teach the perverts.

The first thing Bridget Pendle did was say how she adored the view. Warwick agreed that it was superb and added that he'd miss it.

"Sylvia's been telling me how you stopped them building on that field," said Bridget, indicating Pitts' bare acreage.

"I did my bit," said Warwick modestly. "Of course, it was not easy. Outsiders thought I was exploiting my position for my own benefit, but in politics one soon learns to subjugate one's own feelings and interest for the good of the community. My decision was based on purely environmental considerations."

He sipped his tea and smiled at Bridget Pendle. She had good legs, a firm, trim bosom and the face of a Renaissance beauty, but it was her eyes that entranced the looker. They were deep and brown; a kind of liquid light danced within them, as if continually amused and delighted by what they beheld. By comparison Paula Pomfrey, despite her Titian hair, looked a frump. What had made Pat Pendle want to marry her he could not fathom, or Bridget to... Gawd! He tried to imagine the two women in bed with each other. His imagination boggled.

"I have heard my brother's down here somewhere," said Bridget.

"What?" said Warwick, startled.

"My brother Pat. You haven't run across him, I

suppose?"

"No...no...didn't know you had a brother. Er...mm...did you say he's down here?"

"Tim said he was. That's my other brother. I can't think it's true. Pat hates the countryside."

"There'll be a woman in it somewhere if he is," said Paula.

Warwick shifted uncomfortably. Was he to get no bloody peace of mind? Pat Pendle's presence spelt danger. If he discovered that his sister was engaged in buying Marble Lodge he was hardly likely to keep quiet about what was going to happen to the view she'd been admiring.

"Paula was engaged to him," said Bridget, "but they found out rather quickly that they were really incompatible." She exchanged a smile with Paula.

Sylvia said, "That was lucky – it probably saved you both a lot of unhappiness."

"There's never any point in trying to suppress one's sexuality," said Paula. "However daring the leap, you have to take it if you're going to have any chance of being a complete person."

"People conform to ideas of how life should be lived and suffer for it." Bridget smiled at Sylvia. "They seem to think that making themselves sexually miserable is being good, and what's the point? After all, when you're dead God's not going to say you had a miserable time being good, now go back and enjoy yourself!" She turned to Warwick. "Don't you agree?"

"Er...sex has its place, of course. But..."

"But what is its place? That's the question, eh? With Aids and whatnot, who can answer that, eh?"

"Papa", said Paula, "says that this government has created more prostitutes than any other elected body in recorded history. What do you think of that?"

Warwick smiled bleakly. "I think if he examined a few statistics he would..."

"He hates statistics. He says it's like showing a starving man a menu to prove there's food somewhere."

"Or," said Bridget, "telling a battered wife that most marriages are happy."

Warwick stared at her. Her voice was low and husky. It made his spine prickle. Was it possible it had the same effect on women? If it did it was no wonder Paula Pomfrey had decided very quickly that Pat Pendle wasn't for her. Given a chance and a sex change he was inclined to think he'd have done the same! – though it was a damn shame she wasn't available to be enjoyed as nature intended. That voice...those legs...to say nothing of her tight little bosom. What a waste.

"Warwick!"

He came to with a start. "Sorry what was that?"

"Bridget", said Sylvia edgily, "has asked you twice what you think the chances are."

"Sorry, sorry. Daydreaming. Chances of what?"

"Getting the Humps made into a Site of Scientific Interest."

"What?"

"Papa is organising a petition," said Paula. "It's what the meeting is about."

"Meeting? What meeting?"

"This one. Shelagh's been distributing them. She's interested of course because of her newts."

Sylvia handed him a leaflet. It announced an emergency meeting in the village hall on Saturday to consider local environment issues, with particular reference to a petition being organised to have the Humps declared a Site of Special Scientific Interest. Mr Warwick Tewson, in his capacity as Minister of Rural Affairs and local MP, was expected to be present to answer questions about government policy for the area.

Warwick gazed at it in disbelief. A multitude of questions flooded his mind. The whole thing smelt of conspiracy – a plot to catch him on the hop, force him into a corner. The short notice, the use of the word 'emergency'. Jesus! What was going on? If he went to the meeting he would – but no! He couldn't say anything. That bloody Act again – it even made it secret that it was a secret. There must have been a leak. This was an attempt to see if there was any truth in it. He felt trapped but then, with a politician's instinct for a funkhole, his eye fastened on 'expected to be present'. He hadn't been consulted, or even asked. There was no committal there, no promise he could be held to. He looked up. The three women were gazing at him expectantly.

"I see this is for tomorrow," he said smoothly. "It's rather sudden, isn't it?"

"Papa said you'd understand," said Paula, "as it's your home ground. Your own constituency. He was sure you'd oblige him."

"I'd be happy to," said Warwick. "Unfortunately I have an appointment tomorrow evening – in London."

"Oh dear," said Bridget, her liquid eyes fixed appealingly on his. "Are you sure?"

"Absolutely. Porson reminded me before I left. In fact I almost decided not to come home, but I wanted to see Sylvia."

"But your secretary assured Papa that you never accepted engagements on Saturdays as they spoiled your weekends," said Paula.

Warwick mentally murdered Porson.

"I'm afraid he made a mistake. I definitely have an appointment. I'm addressing the Rural Expansion Group. I can't get out of that."

"But..." Bridget looked at Sylvia, who appeared to

hesitate.

There was an awkward pause. Warwick took it to mean they were expecting her to make a plea on their behalf.

"The arrangements cannot be changed," he said, determined to cut off any argument. "I'm sorry. I would be happy to attend if I could, but affairs of government have to take a precedence over personal wishes."

The woman exchanged uneasy looks, or rather Bridget and Paula did. Sylvia was looking at her feet.

"I really am sorry," he said, mystified by the growing sense of embarrassment, "but it really is an important and long-standing engagement."

Bridget said, "I think we'd better be going, Paula."

Despite pleas to remain they went. Warwick escorted them to the door, repeating his apologies, but their farewells were cool and distantly polite. It did not need a clairvoyant to see that they were distinctly miffed.

"Jesus," he said to Sylvia when he returned to the terrace. "Do they expect me to drop everything and attend a meeting they never even told me about?"

"It's that they know you're lying."

"How the hell can they? Porson isn't God. He forgets things like everyone else."

"Like you've forgotten that tomorrow we're dining with the Breaghs at the Rectory."

Warwick was completely taken aback. "But they don't know that, do they?"

"They do. I told them."

"What!"

"After Sir Archibald telephoned Porson he telephoned me, and asked if we'd be free on Saturday. I told him we were dining with the Breaghs. He then told me about the meeting and said that as the Rector was going to be there after dinner there was no reason why you couldn't be."

Sylvia lifted the tea tray. "Perhaps you'll telephone him now and explain that you can't oblige him."

She went out to the kitchen. Warwick stood still and closed his eyes. He was not a sensitive man but the scorn in his wife's voice was unmistakable, and coming on top of the shock of Sir Archibald's 'emergency' meeting it was too much. He was not going to put up with it! She needed to be told that he was protecting her interests as much as his own. He opened his eyes and walked decisively into the kitchen. Sylvia was stacking the dishwasher.

She glanced at him, said nothing and resumed stacking cups in the dishwasher.

"Look," he said. "There's things need clearing up. We've got to face facts, understand?"

"Will you be going to the meeting?"

"Have to now, won't I? No bloody way out, is there? I'm not blaming you. I can see you just did, well..."

"I told the truth."

"I know you did. I've said, I'm not blaming you, but this business about making the Humps an SSSI. I can't say anything about it – if I open my mouth I'm done for."

"It seems all rather stupid...after all, what's a little tip matter?"

"It matters cos it's going to be bloody nuclear."

Sylvia stopped loading the dishwasher and stared at him. "What?"

"You may as well know. The Humps are going to be used to store the nuclear reprocessing stuff that's being sent back here because the idiots in Ballesfield buggered everything up. Made it unsafe. Jesus! You can see why I had to act quick and sell the house. Who's going to buy a place with nuclear waste stuffed outside the back garden?

"Nuclear...nucl...you..." Sylvia was almost incoherent between disgust and anger. "You knew and said it was just a tip. How could you?"

"I told you – it's this Freedom of Information Act. Even I'm not supposed to know, but now it looks like someone's leaked what's going on. I can't make sense of it! If Sir Archibald smelt a rat he'd hardly be letting his daughter buy this place, would he? Or be selling me Stoke Kirby. He'd be on my neck – but he's the one calling the meeting. It doesn't make sense."

"You are making use of that knowledge to defraud Sir Archibald and you owe your seat to him," Sylvia burst out. "Without his help you wouldn't have got it. Don't you have a conscience about that?"

"You can't afford a conscience in politics. It's too expensive."

"And the people you're supposed to represent as MP. Doesn't it mean anything to you that a lot of them will suffer too?"

"There's no way I can do anything for them. What's going on about making the Humps an infill is nothing to do with me. You know that. I've told you! I had nothing to do with the decision, I wasn't consulted, and there's nothing I can do to stop it happening. All I'm trying to do is get rid of this house before it becomes a millstone round our necks...yours as well as mine...because once that infill's under way it'll be worth peanuts – can you tell me what is wrong with that?"

"You could protest."

"I'd be a voice crying in the bloody wilderness and it'd do me no good. The PM'd probably boot me out and I'd lose money here – can't you see that?"

"Yes, I can see that," said Sylvia. "It's like you are with sex – just thinking of Number One."

"What the...what the hell is that supposed to mean?"

"I don't really know," said Sylvia. "But maybe it's time I thought of Number One."

CHAPTER SEVEN

In a Lather – and Out

It was Mrs Breagh's habit, when upset, to engage in furious bursts of house cleaning. Continual movement of the body somehow stilled the turmoil in her brain, and vicious treatment of inanimate objects liberated the suppressed violence of her heart. These bursts of self-imposed labour were usually accompanied by imaginary conversation in which she reduced the cause of her upset to gibbering submission with a combination of unanswerable logic and devastating wit.

'If you listened to me, Donald, it would never have happened.'

'I always listen to you most attentively, my dear.'

'Then perhaps you can explain to me why you let the bishop use the downstairs toilet!'

Collapse of husband.

Her present activity, however (she was vigorously tidying the boot cupboard by the back door), arose from her daughter's announcement that she would not be dining with the family and the Tewsons that evening as she was dining with a man she had only just met who had rented Pippit Cottage for a month. And they would be dining alone! Mrs Breagh was aghast. The catalogue of dangers she saw in such a foolhardy action included rape, murder, kidnapping, white slavery, abduction, torture and blackmail – to say nothing of the scandal it would evoke locally with her being the Rector's daughter, and the undeniable fact that Vi Ackers, Colonel Necker's daily, had an imagination as vivid as her tongue was long. The mere fact of Shelagh being alone in the cottage with a man...well! Mrs Breagh could not even begin to imagine what Mrs Ackers would make of it. And not only that – there was poor Andrew to consider. How was he going to feel when he heard that his fiancée…

"Ex-fiancée, mother."

"I'm sure if you were to apologise..."

"I have apologised."

"All the same I do think... You have?"

"I met him on the Humps about a week ago. He said he was very sorry."

"He was sorry! Sorry for what?"

"That doesn't matter."

"But you threw the ring at him. Why should he...?"

"Mother, will you please let me sort out my own life? Andrew and I have parted. We are finished with each other. The whys and wherefores do not matter."

"But you can't go dining with a man you hardly know."

"I'm old enough to dine with who I like mother."

In despair Mrs Breagh called on her husband for support but, apart from advising his daughter to be prudent and make sure her nay was nay, as the Apostle Matthew advised, the Rector saw no reason for concern. This was an attitude Mrs Breagh considered unworthy of a father and a Man of God, and said so in no uncertain terms.

"I trust Shelagh because I am both," retorted the Rector, adding somewhat ambiguously, "as I think you should."

"It is the man I don't trust," his wife snapped back irritably. "They do such terrible things, and Shelagh should have more sense than to get herself into positions where they can be done to her – especially as it will make it more difficult for her to get poor Andrew back if he hears that what might happen to her could have, even if nothing had, or she didn't say anything whether it had or not. Which is possible."

The Rector did not attempt to untangle his wife's syntax but dealt with what he felt to be her main concern.

"You must abandon any hope of Shelagh marrying Andrew," he said firmly. "She has made it quite plain that all is over between them."

With that he had retired to his study to complete his sermon on lust, which he intended to deliver the following Sunday.

Abandoned and alone, Mrs Breagh set about venting her annoyance on the boot cupboard, devastating her husband with an imaginary sally that invoked the wise virgins. Shelagh was not so easily defeated, for Mrs Breagh knew that her daughter would pursue her own way whatever was said. Shelagh had an answer for everything, but it wasn't usually to take violent action – which was what made the throwing of the ring at Andrew so mysterious. Of course, it may not have been something he said, but Mrs Breagh refused to let her mind dwell on what he might have done.

Clucking despairingly she rearranged her husband's fine Balmorals. There'd be no more of them now, or any other luxuries. That was another case of Donald ignoring her advice. She had warned him. The man from Blinders, Block & Adams had a wart on his little finger, a certain sign of untrustworthiness. But, as usual, her advice had gone unheeded. She only hoped it would not be the same with Shelagh and this man who obvi... Her train of thought was interrupted by a twinkle of light in the gloom of the cupboard. Mrs Breagh's heart missed a beat. There, stuck in a lump of mud, which must have fallen from a boot or shoe, was the missing ring!

She picked it up. Rubbed it. Dashed to the kitchen and scrubbed it with a nailbrush. Held it in her hand and admired it. Inspected it closely. It was undoubtedly it! The ring! A shining diamond in a neat circle of sapphires. How could any girl resist such a beautiful pledge of love! Surely when Shelagh saw it again she would realise that... Mrs Breagh paused. Was that the wisest thing? The best course of action? No, it was not. To unite the lovers it was necessary to know what the trouble was that kept them apart. Shelagh wouldn't tell...

Andrew might! The ring gave her the chance to have a private chat with him...yes...and perhaps, too, Andrew could persuade Shelagh of the...the...er...that it wasn't wise to go to a cottage with a strange man. Her mind made up, Mrs Breagh went to the telephone. It was a situation that required a mother's touch, a mother's soothing words, a mother's experience...and she was a mother.

The King of the One-night Stands Considers Strategy

Claiming that one is 'not a bad cook' invites the belief that one is really quite a good one. This did not occur to Pat Pendle until he began seriously to consider the cuisine of 'S' for Seduction-of-Shelagh Day. The broad outline of his plan, the order of events, was quite clear in his mind.

A few drinks while they chatted in the cosy intimacy of Pippit Cottage's tiny sitting room; adjourning to the ditto dining room for a delicious meal with a fine vintage wine, followed by a brandy or two and then a casual tour of the cottage to show Shelagh one or two of its architectural oddities (it was, fortunately, blessed with exposed beams and a couple of interesting corbels), ending up in the bedroom where she would, no doubt, be as delighted as he was to find that the bed was a genuine Elizabethan four-poster, covered by an old patchwork quilt that displayed needlework of amazing complexity. And despite the fact that it was unsprung, the bed was remarkably comfortable. Try a bounce on it...oh whoops! Oh dear, they'd fallen over.

From then on nature would take its course and they'd end up doing what nature intended men and women to do. It was a simple plan of proven worth. He had used it, with variations on the attractions upstairs, many times. The current flaw was the meal, a flaw arising not from any weakness in the plan itself but from the fact that Longford Stanton lacked many of the facilities that one took for granted in the metropolis. Like, for instance, those nice, convenient itinerant chefs who were ready to drop everything at a moment's notice and get busy in your kitchen – and disappear just as quickly by the back door when the front doorbell announced the arrival of the guest – thus enabling Pat to greet the lady in his striped apron and brandishing a soup spoon, or some other culinary implement.

To strengthen further the impression of activity in the kitchen he never lingered by the door but gaily begged her to close it, throw her coat somewhere and join him in the galley while he gave the bouillabaisse a final stir. When she joined him there was always a large glass of her favourite tipple on hand to keep the gaiety going as he brought the dish to perfection with something of this or that as prescribed by the departed chef. As starters for a romantic evening it was Pat's opinion that this routine could not be bettered.

Vi Ackers Takes Charge

"There's some Indians wanted to open one of them,"

said Vi Ackers when he asked what cooking services were available. "But they wouldn't hiv anything like that. Not in Longford Stanton."

"I don't mean a takeaway. I mean a chef. A cook who comes in."

"Oh, a cook. You want a cook?"

"Who can come in and prepare a meal."

"Come in the house?"

"That's right."

"Where? In h're?"

"Where else would I want a meal cooked?"

"But I come h're and cook."

"Oh!" Pat eyed Ackers' wife doubtfully. She was small and round-bodied, with a head that looked as if it had been modelled in plasticine.

"But I'm not paid for doing that now. That's part of my job for the Colonel when he's h're, but not when he's not when all I do is do – getting paid only for doing all neat and tidy which I do do as you can see," Mrs Ackers concluded, in a tone that challenged him to deny her success as a cleaner.

"I wasn't asking you to...expecting you to cook for me. I..."

"The Colonel never married," said Mrs Ackers, as if it confirmed the terms of her contract, and added for clarification, "He was in the army."

"Yes, but what I..."

"But now he is in Maidstone with his sister, who cooks for him there, so I don't here."

"No..."

"Except of course if you pay me the right going rate for cooking and it's nothing fancy."

"Ah...er..."

It had not entered Pat's head to consider Mrs Ackers as a possible chef. For the general humdrum needs of a bachelor Colonel she was probably adequate. To prepare a meal to help a bachelor create a mood conducive to seduction needed skills that he felt sure were beyond her. Nevertheless he paused. The situation was critical. It was noon. He had moved his luggage from the Beak and Wedge to Pippit Cottage and found Mrs Ackers already there. She took him on a tour of the premises, pointing out that the Colonel was a very tidy man, left no litter, caused her no trouble, and she hoped Mr Pindle would be the same.

"It's Pendle, Mrs Ackers."

"That's what I said, Mr Pindle, and I hope you understand that housework is hivvy work for thim that has to do it. We wimmin mostly."

Pat promised to keep it in mind. Mrs Ackers evidently had occasional trouble dotting 'e's and 'i's. She then explained everything from how the Aga worked to how the light in the second bedroom didn't because the bulb had gone. While she rambled on Pat congratulated himself on having found such a delightful cottage. It was cosy, comfortable, with well-chosen antique bits and pieces to set off the traditional chintzy furniture. A picture-postcard English country cottage, ideal for romantic dalliance.

Mrs Ackers was putting her coat on and preparing to leave before he thought to question her on the availability of a casual chef, and it soon became clear that he was on a loser. Such things were unheard of in Longford Stanton and Mrs Ackers's tone implied that that was only as it should be.

"I only do plain cooking, mind," she said, as he pondered. "All good, whole and plainsome. Nourishing, and it's four pounds an hour. When would you want it?"

"Well now," said Pat. "I'd like..."

Mrs Ackers cut him short. "Right thin," she said briskly. "It'll have to be something cold. You tell me what and I'll nip round to Killy's an' get it. Only quick, as it's past twilve and I have to get Ackers's, as he's hilpless with food. What about cold ham? Or he does a nice chidder chise...nice with bread and pickle. Or there's pis. Pork, chicken, turkey if you fancy..."

"Please, please, Mrs Ackers. I'm not talking about lunch."

"You're not?"

"It's dinner tonight. I...er..."

"Dinner?"

"Yes, but I think..."

"What time?"

"Sevenish, but there is..."

"That'll be all right then. Ackers will be in the Beak by then so I can oblige."

"Mrs Ackers, I..."

"I'll come in at six – say, quarter to, if you want it sharp on sivin, and you'll want me to do the shopping too, I suppose, it being a menial job and expicted to be done by females. So what have you in mind, Mr Pindle? Bit of biff, lamb chap, liver and bacon, or I can do a casserole, pi – stick and kidney with crusty pastry; and thinn there's veg, potatoes you can have boiled, mashed, fried, roast or sorted – you till me. And pudding. The Colonel was fond of my roly-poly but you might like just chise. You just till me and I'll get it – not that you'll want much being just one."

"I'm not being one," said Pat weakly. "I'm being two."

"Two!"

"I have a guest."

"Ho! Ha...like that, is it?"

"So perhaps," said Pat hurriedly, grasping a straw, "it would be better if...I mean it's probably too much..."

"I can oblige, Mr Pindle. That is a female's job, to oblige. I can do two easy as one. You say what and I'll oblige."

"Well...it's rather, er, special, Mrs Ackers and..."

"You'll have no complaints, Mr Pindle. Just tell me and I'll cook it."

Pat gave up. Shelagh had said she liked home cooking. With some carefully chosen wine, a good plain English meal might be a sound tactical move – and a good conversational gambit.

'I do think French cuisine is overrated. All those ridiculous sauces. They ruin the taste of the meat.'

'I agree. Beef should taste like beef.'

'And, of course, they were originally to hide the taste.'

'Because the meat was rotten.'

'Exactly. We should be proud our ingredients are fresh.'

'Mustard is different. I like mustard with beef.'

'Ah, well that's different. Mustard enhances the flavour.'

'What about hors...?'

"Mr Pindle, I don't have all day," said Mrs Ackers impatiently. "There is Ackers's to get too."

"Oh yes...sorry." Pat returned to the present. "Er...let me see... What did you...?" It was a question of finding what aspect of plain cooking was Mrs Ackers's forte. "You cooked for the Colonel every day, did you?"

"When he was here," said Mrs Ackers with po-faced patience. "He did like to eat ivery day. As I dare say you do, Mr Pindle."

"Quite...quite. But what...er...what was his favourite dish?'

"Licks."

"Licks?!"

"He was very partial to my way of doing licks. His mother was Welsh and he got it from her."

"Ah, leeks...I see. Leeks."

"Specially with my stick and kidney. I do a very good stick and kidney with licks."

"We'll have that then. Yes. Get the best. The very best steak and kidney – and the best li...leeks."

"An' pudding?"

"Er...fruit and cheese. Get some good cheese and fruit."

"Right," said Mrs Ackers. "Money."

Pat fumbled with his wallet and produced two twenty-pound notes. "Will that be enough?"

"I should hope, Mr Pindle. What about the bid?"

"The...the bid?"

"The Colonel always had me turn down the bid when he was entertaining."

"Ah, the bed...well," Pat floundered. He had an overwhelming desire to look down and see if his flies were undone. "I...er..."

"He is a gintleman, old-fashioned," said Mrs Ackers. "But he knew I was open-minded as I am, hiving been brought up to know a woman's place. But no bother, you can till me when I've got the pi in the ovin."

She jerked her coat smartly by the revers and left.

Pat wondered whether Shelagh knew anything of the Colonel's habits. Either way it augured well for the evening. The cottage had the right ambience. Champagne might be in order, but with steak and kidney pie something red and full-bodied might go better – a Fitou, perhaps? Yes. A trip to the local wine store was needed.

Oh Jesus Snoops

In the Beak and Wedge Ackers was arguing with a group of locals when Warwick entered. They looked at him and fell silent, making him feel that he had intruded on a private party.

"Ah, Ackers," he said, with all the affability he could muster. "How are you?"

"Bit like the government," said Ackers. "Still pretending I'm being honest."

"Haha!" Warwick disliked Ackers, but if there was anything one needed to know about the village he was the one to ask. "Tell me, whose is the Ferrari outside?"

"Why, you want to buy it?"

Warwick kept his patience. He'd recognised Pat Pendle's car and it reminded him of how vulnerable he was to an indiscreet word. "Not my style," he told Ackers, "but I thought I knew most cars in the village. Visitor's I suppose, then."

"Could be," said Ackers. "Could be he'll be at Sir Archibald's meeting."

"What?"

"He's interested in newts," said Ackers. "So if anyone strange asks you about 'em you'll know it's him. You'll be there, won't you?"

"Yes, yes, of course. You know him then?"

"I've met him."

"Ah." Warwick sought for a way to learn more but without seeming too curious. "I suppose he's in the hotel, is he?"

"Not in this pub," said Ackers deliberately. "He's rented Pippit Cottage for a bit – wanna know his name too?"

"I don't think so," said Warwick. "I was just puzzled – interested in the car...that's all. Bye."

He'd learned all he wanted to and couldn't get out quick enough

"Bastard," said Ackers and, turning to his companions, he winked broadly. "Better tell the boss."

He went over to the telephone.

Repeated banging on the door of Pippit Cottage bringing no response, Warwick walked round the back and peered in the windows. There was no sign of Pat Pendle.

He returned to the front and considered the matter. Pat was pursuing Shelagh. Shelagh was friendly with Paula Pomfrey who was, who had been, netted by Bridget, Pat's sister – and they were all floating about within a mile or two of each other. Alarm bells, which had been faintly tinkling in his mind ever since Bridget had said Pat was in Longford Stanton, began to ring more loudly. A word from Pat to anyone about the infill and he would be in the shit! Assuming he escaped alive from the baronet's wrath, which was unlikely! It followed therefore that Pat Pendle had to be found and persuaded to leave before he did any damage.

Warwick hurried back towards the village centre. If Pat had left his car at the Beak and Wedge he could not be too far away. Preoccupied with thoughts of how to find him Warwick stepped off the Green right into the path of a large and dirty Rolls Royce.

The sudden blare of its horn caused him to step back quickly. He lost his footing and fell sprawling in a shallow puddle on the verge of the Green. The Rolls, which was travelling quite slowly, halted alongside him and a grey face stared out at him from the driver's seat.

"If you want to commit suicide," it rasped, "there's a pond over there! Try that."

The Rolls drove away. In the doorway of the Beak and Wedge Ackers and friends stood laughing.

Pat Caters

To make sure he could cater for whatever might be Shelagh's favourite drink, Pat bought two bottles of Tattinger, a bottle each of whisky, gin, vodka and Martini, together with tonic, soda water and various fruit juices as mixers. On the vintner's advice he took half a dozen Chateau du Clos Naudin to accompany the steak and kidney pie, a fuller Lafite for the cheese and a couple of Marsala that might be enjoyed with the fruit. As an afterthought he added a bottle each of brandy and crusted port. One could not be too sure.

Satisfied that he had a selection that would make the meal go with a swing and produce that feeling of cosy well-being that he considered a necessary prelude to successful seduction, he arranged for them to be delivered to the cottage by four o'clock. He then set out for the Beak and Wedge, intending to enjoy a light lunch while he mulled over the remaining details of the evening's entertainment. Music was essential and Pat supposed he would have to make do with the Colonel's old deck and a set of LPs that was mostly made up of musical soundtracks. Sinatra's *Songs for Swinging Lovers* might be to the point though. Or how about *Camelot*? Pity the Colonel didn't have *Oklahoma*: 'I'm Just a Girl Who Can't Say No' was exactly the right message.

Pondering, Pat stepped from the cobbled square into the village High Street, and only just avoided being hit by a large and dirty Rolls Royce. He needed no second glance to recognise it, or to know who would be driving. But he was surprised to catch a glimpse of Tim in the passenger seat. He made a movement to call out and stop the car, but was too late. He shrugged and continued on his way to the Beak and Wedge. It was probably something to do with the infill and Tim had come out of curiosity.

Had he been of a more speculative turn of mind Pat would have noted that the Rolls was leaving the village in the direction of Stoke Kirby.

Oh Jesus Snoops Some More

In the hope of learning Pat Pendle's whereabouts and why Sir Archibald wanted a meeting about the Humps,

Warwick called at the Rectory on the pretence of a word with Shelagh. On being told she was not at home he said it could wait till dinner.

"She won't be eating with us, I'm afraid."

"Oh?"

"She's visiting an old friend," said Mrs Breagh brightly. "Who turned up – rather suddenly."

"What sort of friend?" asked Warwick, immediately suspicious. It could be Pat.

"Oh, an old friend from her nursing days." Mrs Breagh was determined that no breath of scandal should touch her daughter. "But tell me, is it true that Paula is buying your house? I do hope so. We shall miss you, of course, but it will be nice to have her as a neighbour. Won't it, Donald?"

"Ummmm," said the Rector, a touch irritably. He disliked being party to a lie but could hardly expose his wife as a liar. But, though irritated, he was interested in the ethical dilemma it posed and noted it as a subject for a sermon. Do we prefer the comfort of lies to the discomfort of truth? Is society itself a lie? The problem had distinct possibilities. Had not John said that lying and the devil were one? Pontius Pilate rules, OK? would make a topical opening .

"Isn't that right, Donald?" His wife's voice broke into his musing.

"Eh?" he said.

"Warwick is wondering why Sir Archie wants a meeting so quickly and urgently about making the Humps a Scientific Site."

"As his daughter is buying your house he is naturally concerned, but it is not simply him. No one trusts Pitts."

"Pitts?"

"Who else?"

It was on the tip of the Rector's tongue to add that no one trusted Warwick either, but he resisted the temptation.

"He owns the field and we all suspect he will continue to try and get Planning Permission to build. He is," continued the Rector with vigour, "an unfortunate symbol of the times. We should all heed Paul to Timothy…'be not greedy of filthy lucre'."

"You mean," said Warwick, "that this is all about Pitts' field?"

"Didn't I tell you I saw a ruffian surveying the place? And did you not promise to report back? Which," said the Rector pointedly, "you have not!"

Warwick ignored the implied censure. "But what has Pitts field to do with the Humps being an SSSI?"

"As it is adjacent to the Humps and has been uncultivated for many years it can be included in the site area. That will effectively prevent Pitts from ever getting Planning Permission. We shall expect you to strongly support us."

A wave of relief swept over Warwick. No need to panic! There had been no leak. No one suspected that anything was going to happen to the Humps. All the fuss was about Pitts field.

"Naturally I will do all I can," he said solemnly. "I will personally present any petition to the Ministry concerned, for – as you may know – the Humps is not my responsibility. But I will be able to assure Sir Archibald and the meeting that Pitts field will not be built on. And no new application has been made."

"Oh that is a relief, isn't it, Donald?" said Mrs Breagh.

"I meant to say, by the way," said the Rector, "that I shall be chairing the meeting. Sir Archibald has had to alter his arrangements for some reason and will be unable to attend."

Warwick almost laughed. Things were getting better all the time.

Old Tom Fancies a Lordship

"Titles," said Sir Archibald Pomfrey, "are accidents of birth or symbols of snobbery...except perhaps for Members of Parliament, who get them as a sort of pension for being 'yes-men'. But you," he turned to Old Tom, who was accepting a pre-dinner whisky, "are not an MP, and certainly not a snob, so why on earth do you want a title?"

"I like the outfit," said Old Tom. "It'd suit me, an' I'd like Dolly to be a lady."

"Tom," said Dolly. "You mustn't say things like that to Sir."

Sir Archibald exchanged an amused glance with Tim. The three Pendles and Sir Archibald were awaiting the call to dinner. Paula and Bridget had been sent to find entertainment elsewhere, Sir Archibald having made it quite clear that he wanted to spend the evening alone with the Pendles.

"He wants to worm something out of your father," Paula confided to Bridget. "To do with the Humps, I expect."

"I'd like to be a fly on the wall then," said Bridget. "Dad's famous for never giving anything away!"

Both daughters had been right. Tom had given nothing away, but Sir Archibald had not revealed exactly what his object was in asking Old Tom and his wife to pay a visit. Ostensibly it was because he wished to meet his daughter's friend's family. The notice had been short but Tim, with an object of his own, had prevailed upon his parents to accept.

Finding that casual questions about the Humps met with non-committal answers Sir Archibald decided to bide his time. Tim's revelation of his father's interest in a title did not immediately suggest itself as a possible way to bargain with Old Tom, but by the time dinner was announced he began to see Tim as an ally. He delayed him at the door of the dining room after Tom and Dolly had entered.

"You'd like your father to have a title," he said. "Am I right?"

"He's sixty-five next year. Be a nice birthday present to go with his pension," said Tim. "Apart from that, I think he deserves recognition. His company performs a public service; he also supports financially a flourishing youth club. A combination of private enterprise and social responsibility that should appeal to this government. He is not a member of the party but I could arrange a substantial contribution to be made to it – would that be enough, do you think?"

"A lot depends," said Sir Archibald, "on who puts his name forward."

"That's what I thought. One needs influential friends."

"I have a few, as I expect you've guessed."

Tim nodded. "On the other side of the coin, I wonder what we have. I know we are Bridget's family, but..." He shrugged and left the question unspoken.

"I'd like your father to do something for me. He might not be willing to do it, but if he did I think I can guarantee his name appearing in the next Honours List. Can I rely on your support?"

"All the way," said Tim. "But I'm afraid you'll never bribe Dad."

"Tush-tush," said Sir Archibald. "He is a businessman and married. He could not have survived in either state without biting a carrot now and then. We'll try it with the port, I think."

CHAPTER EIGHT

Virgin Endangered

"You look absolutely stunning," said Pat.

Shelagh smiled. She was wearing a simple black dress with a silver clasp and carried a small clutch bag.

"Thank you."

"I've got the car outside. This way."

They walked towards the door, Pat conscious that Ackers was standing behind the glass bar partition watching them.

When they got to the Ferrari Shelagh said, "Does this have a catalytic converter?"

"No, not on this model."

"Does it take unleaded petrol?"

"'Fraid not. But it goes like a bullet."

"Do you mind if we walk then?"

"Walk? Why?"

"I don't want to be responsible for polluting the atmosphere."

"But surely...er...well, why not. I like a walk and it's not far."

From behind, at the door of the Inn, Pat heard a muffled snort.

"If it's not far, all the more reason for walking," said Shelagh. She took his arm and an electric charge shot up his spine. "Pollution might not damage us too much at the moment but the effect is cumulative and there's our children to think of."

"Our children!" Pat adopted what he believed to be a tone of amused banter. "That's jumping the gun a little, isn't it?"

"The human race's."

Shelagh smiled up at him. The truth was that for all her coolness and confidence she was feeling distinctly nervous, and when nervous she knew she gabbled.

"It's not only cars and carbon monoxide and the ozone layer – it's the oxygen. If we go on burning things we'll be lucky to survive another thirty years. There'll be no oxygen left to breathe. We'll have used it all up."

Pat dropped his idea of banter and made vague noises intended to convey approval of the sentiment and disapproval of the state of the world.

"Are you really interested in the environment?" she asked.

"Oh yes. Very. It's important. Where would we be without it?"

Before she could answer he added quickly, in an attempt to get the conversation to a more personal level, "You live in a delightful spot, but what's the social life like?"

"Oh there's plenty goes on. Discos in the village hall and lots of groups doing things."

"Ah, yes. I'm sure."

"It's marvellous. We have nature quizzes and plays and games. Guess the Birdie. Things like that."

Pat half suspected she was pulling his leg but she smiled innocently when he looked at her. He dismissed the idea. Guess the Birdie was, after all, no more incredible than most television games. And when one weighed it up, what else was there to do in a village surrounded by nothing but fields?

He squeezed her arm in the first display of affection

that had occurred between them. Shelagh's nervousness increased. There was no doubt in her mind now that Pat had definite intentions regarding how the evening was to develop. It did not really surprise her; what did was that the prospect of being seduced actually rather thrilled her, and her nervousness had its roots in the fear that she might actually succumb – and like it!

Half in fear and half in frolic she gabbled, determined to puncture any atmosphere likely to make her more vulnerable. By the time they reached Pippit Cottage she was well into a lament for poor old Mother Earth, suffocated by a lot of unthinking humans who were really behaving like parasites – perhaps viruses was a better description, for viruses slowly killed off their hosts – not seeming to understand that if we killed off our host, Earth, we'd be killing off ourselves.

"It's so stupid! We can't hop off onto another host like fleas can. When the Earth's gone we've had it."

"Oh, I don't know," said Pat. "We'll probably hop onto another planet."

Shelagh didn't see that working, though she said it could be argued that man was learning to carry his environment with him – like those bugs did when they took a bag of air down in the pond with them, coming up every so often for a refill. On the other hand that's what life had been doing since the start: evolving new bodies to exist in changing environments – like when we came out of the sea – and learning to communicate from inside them.

"Even your car's a new body in a way," she laughed, her nervousness increasing with every step nearer the cottage. "Sending out signals with winking lights and telephones and radios to let others know what you're up to. I dare say," she concluded as Pat opened the cottage door, "that if someone from another planet saw you getting out of your car they'd think you were shedding a skin, like a snake, or like an astronaut when he gets back. Don't you think?"

"I do think," said Pat, beginning to wonder quite what he'd got hold of. "Therefore I am bewildered and need a drink. How about you?"

"Oh yes...yes...that would be nice."

Pat led her into the sitting room, where a log fire was burning, Mrs Ackers having observed that the Colonel always had one. "Hot or cold he always rickoned it hilped things along indoors," she'd said. Pat had to agree. It certainly gave the room a welcoming air.

"I've got everything ready in the oven," he told Shelagh, "so we can enjoy a quiet little drink first."

"How cosy," said Shelagh.

She curled herself up on the rug before the fire, arranging her dress carefully over her knees. "I like fires, but burning fossil fuels is environmentally harmful and very wasteful of energy."

"Don't let it worry you now," said Pat. "What'll you drink?"

"I feel guilty enjoying something I shouldn't. All this waste that is…"

"Never mind the waste," said Pat, determined to get her off the environment. "What about the drink?"

"Don't you ever feel guilty?"

"No I don't, and look," Pat squatted on the arm of one of the easy chairs and looked down at her, "we are not going to be concerned with doom and gloom tonight. We're going to enjoy ourselves, get to know each other. Right?"

He gave her his number one smile, open, frank, honest, charming. He was in his element now. No rain, no newts, no open air, and no other distractions. The food and wine were ready. So was the bed upstairs – and he would go about the business of getting Shelagh there with the practised ease of an expert.

But his smooth, easy charm was switched on so automatically that it awakened in Shelagh a twinge of annoyance. Obviously he thought he had her now, that she would find his charm irresistible and fall into bed, ready to let him enjoy her like a ripe peach.

It also caused her to recall Maggie's appeal that she teach this Don Juan a lesson, and maybe Maggie was right – maybe it was time he learnt that there were women who weren't aching to lie down and let him get on with his fleshly pleasures.

She gave him a dazzling smile. Her nervousness melted away. She knew what she had to do.

"You're sweet," she said. "Let's enjoy ourselves."

"Make a night of it, eh?"

"Yes."

"Throw our bonnets over the windmill!"

"I think they're a neglected source of energy. If we..."

"Shelagh!"

She looked at him, eyes sparkling, as if the mock reproof in his voice thrilled her.

"Let's forget the world's problems," he said, "and concentrate on finding a bit of happiness in each other's company."

"Oh yes. Yes. Let's do that."

"We started off on the wrong foot..."

"Yes, yes, we did a bit, didn't we?"

"But we're going to put that right."

"Tonight?"

"Tonight."

"Wow!" Shelagh gave a half-suppressed gurgle of delight.

Pat began to wonder how she had earned her reputation. It was all going to be too easy.

"So let's kick off with a nice drink to get us in the

mood."

"I think that's a wonderful idea," she said gaily. "Let's do that. Yes, a drink."

"So what's it to be? Whisky? Gin? Vodka? Or champagne – what about champagne?"

"Oh, you've got everything, haven't you?"

"I think I've covered most contingencies, so what'll it be?"

"A glass of water please."

Pat paused. He felt he had been invited to tango and deliberately kicked on the shins, but she was looked at him with such unforced innocence that it was impossible to believe it was intentional.

He smiled. "Surely you can take something a little stronger?"

"Do you think I should?"

"I do, yes."

"Really?"

She returned his smile. He relaxed. She was teasing him.

"It'll warm the cockles," he said, giving her his charming grin. "Make things go with a swing."

"And that's what we want, isn't it. Yes. Really swinging... I will have something stronger. Yes."

"Good. Just name it and it's yours."

"An orange juice."

The warm, pleasurable anticipation suffusing Pat dropped several percentage points. She was either flirting with him or sending him up. This was not the blasé woman who had humiliated him on the Humps, or the blushing virgin who had enchanted him in the square – and, come to think of it, it wasn't the icy young woman who had first excited his interest at the Williams's – and it was very off-putting. How the hell does a man handle a woman who turns on a new character every time he meets her?

He was weighing up how to respond, without showing his irritation and jeopardising his chances of making it with her, when Mrs Ackers put her head round the door and disconcerted him further.

"It's all in the ovin," she said, "and I'm orft."

"I told you to go without bothering us," said Pat, not bothering to hide his irritation.

"Hardly bothering litting you know it's done," retorted Mrs Ackers, ignoring him. "Ivining, Miss Brie, having a good time, are you?"

"Lovely, thank you."

"Listen," said Pat. "Will you..."

"It's one of my stick and kidneys with licks and mash," said Mrs Ackers, ignoring him. "So you'll have a good meal, if nothing ilse."

"Mrs Ackers, w..."

"I'll say good-night, Mr Pindle. 'Night."

Mrs Ackers withdrew but returned immediately.

"Oh, an' I've done the bed, Mr Pindle. I hope it suits you."

She went. Pat fumed, sorely tempted to follow and ram her head in her stick and kidney.

But Shelagh seemed oblivious of the broad hint Mrs Ackers had been intent on giving her.

"She's a sweetie," she said. "Nothing is ever too much trouble for her. You are lucky to have her."

Pat composed his face into a charming smile and agreed. Not wanting to get lost in the drink situation again, he suggested they forget the aperitifs and tackle the steak and kidney right away. Shelagh responded enthusiastically. Mrs Ackers' steak and kidney pies were, she said, a local legend.

The table was neatly and efficiently laid and Mrs Ackers's association with the Colonel evident in the soft lighting, candles burning in an antique candelabrum. The wine, already opened, lay in a basket on the table. Without her parting shot to disillusion him, Pat could almost have been convinced that she was wishing him success.

As if reading his thoughts Shelagh said, "How romantic! Mrs Ackers is doing us proud, isn't she?"

Together they transferred the contents of the oven to the dining room. Pat observed that if the mouth-watering smell lived up to its promise then Mrs Ackers' reputation as a pie-maker would be fully justified. The leeks, too, looked delicious and the mashed potatoes lay in a tureen, under a lump of butter, like a creamy cloud with the sun bursting through. When he plunged the server through the pie crust, rich brown gravy spilled round the dish, a vision of gourmet delight.

"Talk about French sauces," said Pat, remembering his draft script. "What is there to beat English fare at its simple best?"

"It does look good," said Shelagh. "I only hope the meat isn't from some poor hormone-fattened beast that died in agony after being stuffed with chemicals."

The server slipped. A fair portion of diced meat, mushrooms and gravy skidded across the plate and splotched onto the tablecloth.

Shelagh was on her feet at once. She lifted the cloth, grabbed an unused plate and pushed it under the spreading brown stain. Pat stood transfixed.

"I'll fix it," Shelagh said, and disappeared through the door to the kitchen, reappearing almost immediately with a bowl of water, a tea towel and some paper tissues.

While Pat stood speechless, she quickly cleared the mess, reduced the stain to a damp patch of pale brown, removed the debris to the kitchen and returned with a clean plate, which she placed under the stain.

She sat again at the table and smiled at Pat, who had remained silent throughout the whole operation.

"No damage done," she said brightly. "It'll all come out in the wash."

Pat said nothing, gazing at her dumbly, trying to work out what was happening to him.

"Are you all right?" she asked anxiously.

"I was wondering...I think..." He sat in his chair facing her. "Why did you say that?"

"You looked upset so I..."

"Not that! Why did you...? Oh, never mind." He picked up the server. "Only please don't make remarks about...about animals...what happens to animals...just as I'm about to eat."

"But some of the things are really dreadful. Did you know that when they're kill..."

Pat slammed down the server. "I don't want to know. Shelagh, look...listen...I..."

He leaned across the table and looked into her eyes. They were pure, deep blue and sparkled with eager interest, as if nothing mattered at that moment but the words he was about to utter. Desire trickled to his loins, forcing him to close his eyes to regain his composure. He was going to have her. Come what may, he was going to have her.

"Pat."

She touched his hand. The hair on his arm bristled. Pins and needles took possession of his skull. He had known nothing like it since a bob-tailed brunette in the fourth year at St Edmunds had pushed her hand down his trousers to test his boast about pubic hair.

"Are you not feeling well?"

He opened his eyes with a supreme effort, and just about managed to stop himself trembling. When he spoke his voice had a distinct wobble before settling down to its normal, even delivery.

"Listen," he said. "I am as concerned about the state of

the world as the next man. We are putting things into it and taking things out of it so indiscriminately that it's either going to collapse like a punctured balloon or end up as a giant turd before disappearing down some celestial black hole. But it is not something I care to discuss when I'm settling down to an evening with a beautiful woman. So could you please forget about what happened to the steak before it ended up in Mrs Ackers's pie and concentrate on the fact that we are male and female and that the object of the evening is to get to know each other better?"

"Sorry," said Shelagh demurely.

"That's all right. But you do see my point?"

"Oh yes, and I thought you put it beautifully. You really did. Beautifully."

"Good. Now, let's have a glass of wine. It's a Clos Naudin '86, specially selected to go with the steak and kidney pie." Before she could say yes or nay he had tipped a measure into her glass. "Try it and tell me what you think."

She obeyed, gingerly taking a sip as if performing an act of great daring to please him. Having swallowed it she smiled.

"It's very nice," she said.

"Good," he said and filled his own glass. "Let's drink to us, shall we?"

"Yes, let's."

They clinked glasses and drank, looked into each other's eyes and smiled. Pat's sense of well-being returned. The evening was on the right track again.

"Now for the steak and kidney," he said, and plunged the server into the pasty. "This time it's going to stay on the plate."

"Of course," said Shelagh, "alcohol is a kind of poison really. In the stomach it..."

"Shelagh!"

She stopped. He wagged the server at her reprovingly.

"The rule is – conversation on personal matters only."

"Sorry."

"Tell me about yourself. What do you do?"

"I've done several things: trainee nurse, but I gave it up as I can't bear seeing people suffer; then I was learning about antiques and gave that up..."

"Why? It's a very good business."

"It's too cheaty, it really is...and so pseudo and arty. What do you do?"

"I'm sort of in the City." He handed her some pie on a plate. "Nothing very exciting."

"You're just a well-dressed gambler then."

"Ha ha, I suppose so in a way." They settled down to eating, helping themselves to vegetables. "But it's a living."

"It's not doing anything useful though, is it? It doesn't produce anything – just playing with money to make money."

"All right, so it is," said Pat. "Nothing wrong in that, is there?"

"Do you have haemorrhoids?"

Pat choked. Only a quick movement of his hand stopped the food in his mouth from returning to the plate. He rose to his feet and staggered coughing round the room, his face crimsoning as he tried to regain his breath. Shelagh took his arm and thumped him on the back. A shower of half-masticated food shot from his mouth and spattered on the wall.

"Jesus Christ," he gasped. "Don't do that!"

"But Pat..."

"For God's sake!" He sank into a chair, still coughing. She offered him a glass of wine but he waved it away.

She sat opposite him, watching anxiously as the

paroxysm subsided and he took in great gulps of air, his mouth agape with the effort. Finally his breathing became more or less normal and he sat, chest heaving, mouth open like an exhausted runner at the end of a bitterly contested race.

"That was bad," said Shelagh solicitously. "Did something go down the wrong way?"

"What in the...what..." Pat fought for words to express his angry bewilderment. "What the hell are you up to?"

"Me?" Shelagh widened her eyes in surprised innocence.

"Yes, you. Every time we seem to be getting somewhere you torpedo it."

"But Pat, I don't understand. Where are we supposed to be getting?"

He gazed at her blank-eyed, took a long drink of wine, left his chair and paced up and down the room, occasionally glancing at her as she sat watching with an expression of deep concern that both attracted and baffled him.

"Why did you ask if I had haemorrhoids?" he said at last.

"You said we should get to know each other."

"But for God's sake," he expostulated, "you can't ask people things like that out of the blue in the middle of a meal. It's...it's...I'm damned if I know what it is, but it's just not done. Such things are personal, private, don't you understand that?"

"But I thought you wanted to talk about personal things, so that we'd get to know each other better."

"You can't be that innocent," he snapped, losing patience. "You must know damn well I didn't mean that sort of personal."

"I'm sorry," Shelagh said demurely. "You should have explained."

"What do you mean, 'explained'?" he demanded, his

voice rising almost to a falsetto with disbelief. "Did you expect me to say let's have a personal chat but don't mention my haemorrhoids?"

"You do have them then?"

"I do not have them!"

"But Pat, you said don't mention my haem..."

"In God's name! It doesn't matter whether I have them or not. You don't ask people about that sort of thing. It's not done."

"Well I think it should be. If you have haemorrhoids you should..."

"I do not have haemorrhoids!"

"Are you sure? You're not just being..."

"Of course I'm bloody sure," he shouted, now thoroughly rattled. "Do you want a certificate or something?"

"No, that's sil..."

"I do not have haemorrhoids, so can we now forget about them?"

"I only asked because I'm interested in diet and city men drink a lot of alcohol, which is very constipating and causes..."

"Jesus Christ – have you got an anal fixation or something?"

"I don't think so. That's a masculine fixation, usually, though whether it's the anus or the faeces that..."

Pat banged the table violently. She stopped. There was a tiny pause. He glared at her.

"I'm sorry," she said. "Men don't like talking about these things – do they?"

Pat struggled to speak calmly. "We're supposed to be having a romantic evening, so you tell me my car is poisoning the atmosphere, then it's something I put on like a snakeskin or astronaut's overcoat to go to the goddamn moon and back.. Then it's orange juice, animal hormones, haemorrhoids, constipation and bottoms generally – what the hell! What's next on the agenda? Ingrowing toenails?"

"Sex, I expect," said Shelagh.

"Oh good," he snorted unthinkingly. "Then I suppose we...ah..." The word registered. He stared at her.

She smiled. "You'd like that, wouldn't you?"

He eyed her warily. She was altogether too calm, too innocent-looking, too demure – and he no longer trusted his judgement of her.

"Just what are you up to?" he asked. "You're playing some sort of game with me. What's the idea?"

"I'm wondering if your diet includes br..."

"Never mind my bloody diet or the state of the world..."

"But you said yourself that you were concerned..."

"I'm not now. Right now all that concerns me is why you're playing me like a cod on a hook."

"I'm very fond of cod. It's very nutritious and if you do have haem…"

"God damn and blast! Shut up...just shut up!"

"But Pat..."

"I said shut up...shut up or I'll brain you with the bloody pie dish!"

"Very well, Pat." Her blue yes were limpid and apologetic. "I don't want to upset you and spoil our evening together."

Pat gave up. He sat in his chair, head bowed, like a frustrated naughty child who had been denied a lollipop, and gazed dumbly at the tablecloth. The pale brown stain resembled the big toe of Italy and he found himself remembering a childhood rhyme:

Great big Italy kicked little Sicily
Into the Mediterranean Sea;
Up jumped Asia, said he was Hungary,

Took a bit of Turkey and dipped it in Greece.

Shelagh was moved to pity him. She had driven him hard. Perhaps she had gone too far. He needed comforting. She got up and went to him.

Out of the corner of his eye Pat saw her approach. She stood close and started to stroke his hair gently. First with one hand and then the other, then both, moving from forehead to crown, rhythmically, caressingly.

A shiver ran through him. She was aggravating, frustrating – but intoxicatingly female and made him tremble with desire. Maybe he could still get her. For all that had been said of her reticence she was not shy – and all the indications were that, despite her barmy conversational embarrassments, she wanted him. It was simply a matter of getting her in the right mood, and if she wanted to comfort him...maybe she was asking for it now!

He let his head roll to one side, resting against her stomach. Beneath her dress material, the flesh was warm and yielding. Looking down he saw the firm outline of her thighs below the curve of the mons Veneris. His mouth went dry. Her hand was now caressing his ear. Tweaking it from behind, bending it forward then letting it fall back as her hand returned again to stroke his hair. Dear God, she's asking for it, he thought! Must be! Cautiously he let his hand drop and touched her knee. She stiffened but continued to stroke her chair.

"You want to go to bed with me, don't you?"

He said nothing.

"It's what you brought me here for, isn't it?"

It was too good an opening to miss. He looked up at her. Her eyes were calm, there was a faint trace of a smile on her lips. She moved her hands down from the crown of his head and cupped his face.

"Is that so wrong? You're a beautiful woman. I'm a

man. It's how things should be."

It was a line he had delivered many times before but this time he could not help feeling that he sounded like a child appealing for a favour.

"You're quite handsome yourself," she said, and unable to stop herself, added, "But what if you've got genital warts or something?"

He wrenched her hands from his face and jumped furiously to his feet, pushing her back so violently she staggered against the sideboard, rattling the Willow Pattern plates and dishes. But he was beyond caring. She had done it again – conned him into thinking that her guard was down, then belting him one in the solar plexus.

This time he did not shout at her. He stopped himself in time, stilled his rage and advanced on her like a predatory stoat on a rabbit. He pressed his abdomen close to hers, imprisoning her against the sideboard. She leaned backwards, distancing her face from his, and he was gratified to see a glimmer of alarm in her eyes.

"I've got a condom," he said quietly. "So what about it?"

"How do I know there's not a hole in it?" she said, the slightest of trembles in her voice.

"It's a risk you have to take."

He was deliberately menacing. He eyed her bleakly, then pulled her to him and pressed his lips against hers. She struggled furiously, but he held her close and she began to yield, and what began as a forced kiss ended up as a passionate embrace.

She was half-laughing, half-protesting as they sank slowly to the carpet, rolled over and over, coming to rest only when he managed to scramble astride her, pinning her arms to the floor with his forearms while he held her head steady between his hands. She stopped struggling and lay beneath him, her chest heaving, her lips slightly parted with the effort of breathing, her eyes fixed on his.

There was such stillness between them that each could feel the thump of the other's heart. For Pat it was a moment of unbearable anticipation, quite unlike the desperate urgency of sexual arousal he had known with other women. It was something more than ordinary desire. It was a sense of coming fulfilment when they could both lose themselves in the sheer, uninhibited physical union that twin spirits alone can know. Unthinkingly, instinctively responding to impulses buried deep in his sexual being, he began to move his pelvis gently and rhythmically, caressing her with a slow, circular movement until she began to respond with a forward thrust, her legs slowly opening to welcome the consummation of mounting passion.

Naked, their coupling would have been inevitable, but naked they were not. Pants, trousers, knickers and tights needed to be removed and, while it may be true, as countless films and ad-men would have it believed, that sexual passion in full flight is so unstoppable that partners will tear every vestige of clothing from each other in their haste, Shelagh was an exception.

As Pat's sexual temperature reached fever pitch he ceased his pelvic gyrations to lift her dress and tear feverishly at her knickers. The movement shattered the spell, allowing what had been a still, small voice in the fire of desire to become a yelp of protest.

"No...no...no," she cried. "You mustn't do that."

"Shelagh darling..."

"Don't darling me. I'm not one of your easy lays."

"It's not like that, Shelagh. I..."

"You boasted to Jimmy Williams that you'd get me."

"Shelagh, I don..."

"Don't deny it. It's why you came here. Maggie told..."

"Blast Maggie. Listen, I love you... I do... Kiss me and you'll know it's true."

He managed to force his lips to hers but she rolled over and managed to tear herself free. Grabbing at a chair she hauled herself to her feet. His hand was still holding her knickers and they descended to her thighs.

"Let me go. Let me go."

He rose beside her, releasing her knickers and, getting his arms round her waist, pressed his lips firmly against hers. He felt her respond – as she did so he was wrenched away from her and twisted round.

Crump!!

Something like a battering ram hit him in the face. He went careering backwards into the sideboard. A shower of Willow Pattern plates and dishes fell around him and he sank to the floor.

The room was filled with stars and dancing coloured lights. He was dimly aware of someone daubing his face with a wet cloth and there were loud voices. The lights began to recede. Shelagh was saying something. A deeper male voice replied, plaintively, it seemed. Then his head cleared and Shelagh's face was immediately before his.

"Pat darling. Sweetheart, wake up," she was murmuring frantically. "Please, please, for my sake."

"What the hell!"

He tried to get to his feet. Shelagh put her arm round him, trying to help, but his knees refused to cooperate. "What happened?"

"Are you all right?"

"Something hit me." He held drunkenly onto the sideboard and blinked, still dazed. "Did the roof fall in?"

"It was Andrew."

"Who?"

"Andrew. I'll make it up to you. I'll send him away and we can be together properly."

"Don't be stupid, Shelagh. Your mother is quite right. You shouldn't be here with him."

Behind Shelagh a square-jawed man in a blazer came into focus. The face vaguely familiar

"What...?" said Pat stupidly. "Where did he come from?"

"You were trying to rape her," said the man, staring fixedly at Pat. "That's not a thing a gentleman does."

"He was not trying to rape me," said Shelagh.

"Then why were you shouting 'No...no' and 'Don't' then?"

"That's none of your business."

"Your knickers were round your knees."

"You had no right to come barging in, wherever they were." Shelagh stroked Pat's face. "Oh poor darling. You've got a bad bruise."

"Just a minute, just a minute." Pat put down her hand. "He came in and socked me because he thought I was raping you?"

"I'll make it up to you, Pat. It was mother, you see..."

"He was on the Pudden, wasn't he?" said Pat, the square jaw jolting his memory. "You kissed him and cocked your leg up."

"That's all over, Pat. I'm yours now."

"You're what?"

"You know what I mean." She kissed his face radiantly, her eyes shining. "We'll send him away and start again. We..."

"Like bloody hell!" said Pat violently. "You can get out and take Sir Galahad with you."

"Just take me in your arms, Pat, and you'll see what I..."

"I know what I'll see! It'll be your mother leading the cavalry in to save your virginity. Well, they are welcome to it. So is he." Pat nodded at Andrew. "If he hasn't already had it for afters on the Pudden."

"That's not fair, Pat!"

"What's fair about prick-teasing? Codding a man along till he's all worked up then giving him a cold douche."

Shelagh went bright pink. "That's an awful thing to say."

"Let's teach him a lesson." Andrew advanced on Pat but Shelagh stopped him.

"No, he's not worth it. He doesn't think of women as human. To him they're just sex objects to be lusted after."

"Christ," said Pat. "Do you think women paint themselves to stop men looking at them? No, don't tell me. Get back to your newts. You haven't grown up yet."

"At least newts don't pretend to be peacocks."

"When the nuclear waste gets dropped on them they might. So hop it and enjoy them while you can."

Shelagh and Andrew exchanged a look.

"What are you talking about?" said Andrew.

"Go away," said Pat. "I have an immoral longing in me and need a rest."

Andrew grabbed him by the shirt. It was apparent that he was immensely strong. Shelagh made no attempt to stop him this time and he placed a large fist under Pat's chin.

"Tell or have another," he said. "What's this about nuclear waste?"

"They're going to stuff the Humps with it. Any more pulling on the Pudden will be radioactive – now drop me, do you mind?"

Andrew tightened his grip. "If it's true, how is it we've heard nothing about it?"

"It's an Official Secret. In fact it's so official and secret no one's even supposed to know it's a secret."

"Then how do you know?" The fist threatened again.

"We're doing the dumping. Pendle's Disposal. We

shift the shit of civilisation. Satisfied?"

Andrew released him and turned to Shelagh.

"Ackers said there was something on. It's why Tewson is selling his house, but nuclear...oh, my God!"

Shelagh's face was white. She turned to Pat. "When are they due to start?"

Pat shrugged. "Ask Ackers, he seems to know everything."

Andrew made a move. Pat stepped back hurriedly but Shelagh intervened.

"Let's go," she said to Andrew. "I feel sick."

"Not half as sick as Tewson's going to feel," said Andrew. "Let's get to that meeting and get the truth out of him."

"You've no chance," said Pat. "He'll hide behind the Freedom of Information Act."

"Information bollocks! If he doesn't come clean we'll lynch him!"

Andrew put his arm round Shelagh and they made for the door.

Shelagh turned and gave Pat a reproachful look before leaving, her face no less beautiful for the hurt in her eyes.

And for once in his life Pat wished he was a he-man. A he-man strong enough to flatten Andrew senseless, and do unto Shelagh everything a frustrated primitive he-man could and would!

Oh Jesus hits trouble

All was going well for Warwick Tewson. He was not an accomplished orator. Rousing speeches was not his forte, but he was a skilled equivocator and found no difficulty in telling the meeting in Langford Stanford Village Hall that responsibility for the Humps and Pitts field did not come within his remit as Minister of Rural

Affairs. If plans did exist he would not be privy to them, nor would he expect to be.

His listeners could be assured, however, that he would do everything in his, admittedly limited, power to support their wish for the area to be designated an SSI. He also wanted to save Pitts field from the depredations of speculative builders. Low-cost housing would lower the tone and desirability of the village and, a local resident himself, he was as eager as they were to preserve Longford Stanford as a haven of peace and dignity.

Someone in the hall pointed out, sourly, that as he was moving to Stoke Kirby he wouldn't be a resident for long.

Warwick was excusing the move with all the sincerity of a conman trying to close a deal when Andrew Hawkins, with Shelagh hot on his heels, strode up the central aisle shouting, "You're a liar! A hypocrite! You're selling up because you know a load of nuclear waste is going to be dumped on the Humps which your house overlooks." Turning to the meeting Andrew went on, "Talk about sleaze! He is using inside knowledge of government plans to feather his nest while the rest of us will be left to suffer the consequences of living next door to a nuclear dump! I challenge him to deny it!"

The suddenness of the assault hit Warwick like a kick in the mental genitals. In the stunned silence that followed Andrew's outburst he struggled to regain his wits, but only managed to squeak like a frightened mouse as the meeting erupted in a torrent of shouted questions.

Pandemonium followed.

CHAPTER NINE

Mucktrading

In the drawing room Old Tom accepted a cigar and Dolly took a glass of port. It was a pleasant evening and they sat by the open French windows looking across lawns to a sunken garden. Beyond the trees that fringed the valley in the middle distance the last faint crimson of sunset could be seen.

"It is lovely," said Dolly. "Like a postcard."

"Nice colour for a dress," said Tom. "You ought to get one like it. An' it reminds me," he turned to Sir Archibald, "that was blackberries in the tart, was it?"

"You liked them?"

"I was tellin' Dolly, wasn't I, Doll? Funny how blackberries come up red." Tom puffed his cigar and sent a curl of blue smoke wafting through the window. "Nature can be like that. Never know where you are with it. Mind, I'm a city man born and bred, never had much liking for outdoors in fields and that, but I could settle here. Must be age, I suppose; getting soft."

"Be nice," said Dolly, "to have a country cottage. We could run down weekends. Like we used to to Southend."

"But you might be safer in London," said Sir Archibald.

"Oh, get on, sir," said Dolly. "You don't have muggings round here. There's no one to do it. Is there, Tom?"

"I reckon," said Old Tom shrewdly, "as it's not muggin's as Archie is worried about."

"What do you think is worrying me, Tom?"

"You tell me. I haven't any worries. I've a cigar, a drink and a full belly. What more can I want? Or you, either?"

"If you got back home and found the government was planting a bomb – a nuclear bomb – at the end of your street, would you be worried?"

"I'd shift," said Tom. "It's a free country."

"That's not an option open to everyone."

"Hard luck – just the way the dice falls."

Tim, who had been listening carefully, seized his cue. "Surely they're not doing anything nuclear around here?"

"Maybe," said Sir Archibald. "A short while ago I was told by a friend in Whitehall that the very deep hole on Stanton Humps was being examined for use as an infill of some kind. I made enquiries but no one seemed to know anything about it. Apparently, though even this is not admitted, it is covered the Freedom of Information Act. As far as the media are concerned, Stanton Humps have ceased to exist."

"What a funny thing," said Dolly.

"Tragic, I'd say. The Humps are a beauty spot and, although I can't find out for certain what's going to be put there, I suspect it will be nuclear...or something just as bad. But I can't mount a campaign against it until I find out exactly what is going to happen. The contractor doing the infilling must know and could..."

"Archie," Old Tom cut in, quietly but emphatically. "I've taken to you. You've got no side, but you're in the clouds. I've spent my life shifting shit – you might not like the word but that's what it is, shit. And who makes it? People. Who don't like it dumped on their doorstep or back yard? People! Do you know, Archie," Tom leaned forward and stubbed out his cigar in an ashtray on the coffee table, "I saw it coming years ago, which is why I'm in the business, but I never thought it'd get like it is... We're living on a great dung heap, all of us, but how many of the people who dump it do anything to make it less of a dung heap? Do you? No, you don't, leastways not if your dustbin's anything to go on. I took a look. Trained eye, see, professional interest... Not as you're any worse than the rest of 'em – all wanting what they want and having it, and leaving it to buggers like me to get rid of. And if I have to spoil a bit of pretty countryside doing it I am not bothered. Know why? Cos the cities are filthy enough as it is – and who made 'em filthy? Why, the wealthy buggers who don't care to live in 'em, and squeal when a bit of the shit they've been living off lands in their own back yard. No offence, nothing personal, but it's how it is." He got up from his chair. "I'm off to bed, but just one thing – being used to shit – if I get to being a Lord in Parliament, I'll feel quite at home. 'Night."

"Well," said Dolly, as the door shut on Tom. "Fancy. I've never heard him like that before, but he always is a bit funny away from home. I'd better go and see to him."

Dolly hurried out of the room. Tim and Archibald looked at each other.

"Drink?" said the baronet.

"What I don't understand", said Tim, nodding acceptance, "is quite what you expected from Dad. There's nothing he could do, apart from telling you a start date and what's being used for the infill. He couldn't stop it taking place."

Sir Archibald smiled and handed him a brandy. "That all right?"

"Fine, but..."

"This Freedom of Information Act is being used to keep anyone from knowing what is planned for the hole.

Our only chance is the infilling contractor – he must know what's being dumped." He lifted his glass. "Cheers."

"You won't get anything out of Dad."

Sir Archibald shrugged and drank.

Tim said, "Tewson's house overlooks the Humps. If you think the infill's going to be dangerous why are you buying it?"

"To thwart him. The sale, if it happens, won't be completed until I find out exactly what is going on. The man's completely amoral, beyond even what one normally expects from a politician and I'm sure he's selling because he..."

The telephone rang. Sir Archibald picked it up, identified himself and then listened in silence, only occasionally emitting a grunt of understanding or agreement.

Finally he said, "It's too good to miss, Ackers! Get right off to the meeting and if they don't push Tewson you do it, understand? Ask about the house – the press'll be there, so...well, use your head but don't let him off the hook. Yes, bye." He put down the phone. "The dump at the Humps", he told Tim, "is going to be radioactive waste from the Pollocks and maybe chemical waste as well."

"Who says?"

"Your brother told the Rector's daughter not ten minutes ago. He's been dating her, or whatever's the word for it nowadays."

"One-night stands with him, I'm afraid," said Tim. "He's a dedicated freebooter."

"Mmmm." Sir Archibald drummed his fingers on the desk. "If I know anything of Shelagh he'll be getting the booting but, more importantly, I doubt your brother would make a statement about what's going in the Humps unless he did know. After all, it's your father's firm so he should know, shouldn't he?"

"Not necessarily. I'm on the board and I didn't know. We're just there for decoration and a good salary."

"That's as maybe, but it would be difficult for either of you to prove that you didn't know what was going on."

"Does it matter?"

"In certain circumstances it would. Ah...ah... Help yourself to another drink, Tim, I'll be back in a moment."

In his study Sir Archibald rang Scotland Yard, asked for Assistant Commissioner Roberts, an old friend, and told him that a serious breach of the Freedom of Information Act had been committed in Longford Stanton.

Oh Jesus cops it in the Stocks

Warwick Tewson, recovering his wits, managed to restore at least a semblance of order to the meeting but refused to confirm or deny Andrew's accusation that the Humps were to be used as a site for nuclear waste disposal, repeatedly insisting that he was ignorant of any plans, that it was none of his business and even if it had been, the Freedom of Information Act would prevent him telling them.

Irritation at Tewson's stonewalling tactics culminated in someone in the crowded hall shouting, "Put him in the stocks. That'll get the truth out of him."

Carried away by collective frustration the normally complacent well-heeled villagers responded enthusiastically to the call and bundled the loudly protesting MP to the historic place of shame; only a deep-rooted instinct for political survival kept Warwick from crying quits. He was frightened almost out of his wits but revealing the government's plans would get right up the PM's nostrils – a decidedly unrewarding place for any ambitious politician – whereas suffering indignity to preserve the integrity and good name of the government would surely invite, nay deserve, a substantial expression of thanks.

But even an instinct for political survival has limits; it needed only a volley of old cabbages, ripe fruit and a splattering of eggs from the ruder villagers for Warwick Tewson to reach his. He'd tell all if only they'd calm down and listen!

Pat Looks on the Bright Side

Pat Pendle was far from happy. He bathed and tried to relax. His jaw ached but worst of all, a kind of dull hurt was bothering the region of his left ribs, and he was uneasily aware that it had to do with the thrill that had electrified him while atop of Shelagh. It was not lust; lust he had experienced many times, and it was nothing to the excruciating desire that Shelagh had awakened in him.

Pat was far from being a sentimentalist; never given to romanticising what went on between men and women, love was an emotion alien to his lifestyle. Love meant surrender; it created obligations and responsibilities that would severely curtail the carefree existence he cultivated so assiduously – and successfully, except for that one terrible error with Paula. He'd been more or less drunk at the time and...but why bother with that? There'd been no feeling involved there. This...well, this...this Breagh female, from what he'd heard, took it all seriously. Very seriously. Love to her meant involvement, concern for feelings and the future, belief in the worth of sacrifice. Commitment! Pat shuddered involuntarily. His philosophy was sex yes, commitment never. Happiness was primarily distancing. In a nutshell – keeping apart. The risk was not that lovers never got to know each other – they got to know each other too well. There was no magic in propinquity – the closer the eye the coarser the grain.

What had happened was probably for the best. Of course it was! He could almost thank Andrew or whatever his name was for socking him in the jaw. Had that thrilling moment with Shelagh been prolonged he might easily have succumbed to the lure of legal possession and ended up in the net of matrimony. He came out in a cold sweat. Jesus! There was a time for man to run – and this was it!

He packed his bags, kicked the four-poster and set out to collect the Ferrari from the Beak and Wedge car park. The sooner temptation was behind him, the better.

Legal Complications

Pippit Cottage was off a little-used minor road joining Longford Proper to Longford Stanton, but as Pat turned into it there was shouting from towards the village and several cars flashed by in quick succession.

When he reached the Green it was thick with parked cars and people milling noisily round the far side of the duck pond. He could not see the cause of the excitement but on the steps of the Beak and Wedge he met Ackers.

"What's going on?" he asked.

"They've got Tewson in the stocks," said Ackers, grinning broadly.

"Good grief. What's he done?"

"They wanna know why he put his own house up for sale without letting on as there might be dumping nuclear stuff on the Humps. Mind," continued Ackers with contempt, "they'd have all done the same in his shoes. Middle-class bastards."

"Does he...er..." Pat repressed a twinge of guilt; his outburst to Shelagh and her bullyboy was probably responsible for Tewson's plight. "Why won't he tell them?"

"Who knows?" Ackers grinned. "But he keeps saying

he can't say anything cos Freedom of Information won't let him."

"Well, that's true," said Pat.

"Well, him saying it's only made it worse cos somehow it's got about", Ackers' grin broadened, "as there's going to be a service road through the village to take the stuff up to the Humps." A shout went up from the crowd. "Hark at 'em! There's nothing worse'n the middle classes dealing with what they thinks is traitors to their lolly – and talking of lolly there's a couple of gents eyeing your Ferrari like they think it ought to be theirs."

Pat hurried to the Inn park. He saw no one, but as he unlocked the car two men emerged from the shadows.

"You Mr Patrick Pendle?" said one.

"What if I am?"

The man produced a card and held it up for inspection. "We'd like you to come along with us," he said.

CHAPTER TEN

Oh Jesus Crucified

The Minister of Rural Affairs' political career was saved by the siren wail of a police car, but he could not avoid the resulting publicity. Fellow MPs expressed sympathy and sniggered in the bars; he knew it and inwardly seethed but advised, or rather ordered, by the PM he treated the incident as a huge joke.

"Schoolboy stuff," he told interviewers. "No, I won't be taking any action. A lark that got out of hand, that's all. Forget it."

The press echoed the joke in jokey headlines. 'MINISTER EGGED ON!' bellowed the *Sun*, 'MP SHOCKED IN THE STOCKS', screamed the *Mirror*. The *Mail* could only manage 'RURALS REVOLT!' as its banner; slightly smaller type advised readers to turn to page three for a woman's view of a most un-English act.

The broadsheets essayed slyer humour: the *Guardian* featured a Bell cartoon showing Tewson in the chamber, his head decorated with rotting fruit, dismissing fears about genetically modified crops. *The Times* chose 'STOCKS AND SOCKS'. Only the *Independent*'s headline touched on the original purpose of the meeting with 'NEWTS TO BE NUKED?' in careful quote marks to avoid possible prosecution.

Questions were asked but there were no answers: commercial confidentiality was involved so the Freedom of Information wouldn't allow any.

The blanket of silence that met their enquiries affronted the Longford Stantonians' sense of their own importance and, like the MP they reviled, the prospect of financial loss spurred them to action. They were not going to let the value of their cosy, costly nooks be reduced without a prolonged and, if necessary, bloody fight. A committee was formed, plans made and watches set up. At the first sign of any suspicious activity the classy inhabitants all swore to lie in the roads and lanes to prevent the movement of lorries.

Meanwhile estate agents received an unusual number of instructions, which were, of course, to be kept strictly confidential.

Pat Pendle's arrest passed unnoticed in Longford Stanton, except for Mrs Ackers who had the job of clearing up Pippit cottage.

"Ho," she said to Mr Ackers the day after Tewson's ordeal in the stocks, "there has bin goings on ilsewhere too! Mr Pindle's not here any more, he isn't, having gone without saying and a fin mess leaving bihind too. I shall have to be ripporting it to the Colonel as how his china hirelooms is damaged which he won't like and'll have to be pied for. And what's more thire's has been no sleeping in the bid which means something or not as the case may bi."

Her husband kept his counsel as to the reason for Pat's going, but asked what the 'something' was.

"Such as he didn't get his way with hir like min try to with wommin."

"You don't need a bed for that," said Ackers.

"To do goings on with Miss Brie you would," said Mrs Ackers, "an' it's my opinion he had high hipes with them clin sheets…poor dir! How that room was she like had to fight him off hard."

"Led him on, wanted it, then lost her nerve, I expect,"

said Ackers. "Virgins are like that."

Sex has its Attractions

Shelagh was in emotional turmoil; so was red-speckled *Triturus cristatus*. She watched as it erected its high spiky crest and turned itself 'U' shaped, whipping its tail in sexual frenzy to persuade a female to slide over his ejaculated spermatophore. It didn't seem much fun for the female, though it could be that she got quite a thrill from being lashed about a bit by the male's tailpiece. But, fun or not, how much easier sex was for them! When they wanted it they didn't think of resisting temptation, they just got on with it – and Pat Pendle had the same idea. Almost the first thing he'd said to her was "Come to bed with me."

Knowing this, why on earth had she walked wide-eyed into his cottage as if asking for it? Made a complete fool of herself and...oh God! She crimsoned at the thought of it...the humiliation of being rescued with her knickers half down by a man she'd rejected for putting a hand up her skirt. She mentally castigated herself. How could she have been so stupid? How could she have let herself be so carried away? Stupid, stupid, STUPID!

Maggie had warned her...but oh God!...the ecstasy...the exhilarating thrill of desire that invaded her body when he touched her... She had wanted him more than words could tell, ached for him so passionately that the long-held resolve that her sexual initiation would never be anything but a celebration of married love had evaporated. Every reservation, ideal, thought, sense, feeling, principle – everything humankind had invented or evolved to conceal and control its animal nature had been trampled out of existence by the overwhelming, primitive desire to mate; every instinct urging her to respond, to yield to the deliciously compulsive urge to unfold like a flower beneath him and do it!

Only Andrew's arrival had prevented Pat Pendle chalking her up as another conquest. And it would have meant nothing to him. He took sex as casually as the red-speckled warty newt, expecting women to do the same, and they mostly did. All her friends talked of sex as if it were nothing more than the sweet course of a good meal. Some even boasted of their conquests much as, according to Maggie, Pat Pendle did. Virginity and chastity didn't concern them; all it needed was a male to thrash around them a bit and they were at it like the newts whereas she... Well, Shelagh told herself fiercely, her friends could behave like animals if they wished! She wasn't a newt, and she had no intention of behaving like one. Humans were different – they cared for each other: no female newt would bother to warn another to watch out for an old warty who wanted to lay her and leave her, as Maggie had warned her about Pat Pendle. But then newts had no social or moral problems about sex. They did it unthinkingly with only one object, one purpose, and once done it was finished with. But humans were at it all the time, frustrating its purpose in pursuit of pleasure. Well maybe she was old-fashioned, still under the influence of her father's religious teaching but, whatever other women thought, she did not see her body as a sort of pleasure playground, readily available to any friendly male who fancied it. She wanted it to be honoured, treasured, offered as an act of love. Was that something to be derided? Laughed at? Sex was a funny business, no doubt about that and...

Shelagh eyed the red-speckled warties speculatively. They were still thrashing about in a kind of ritual dance. Were they experiencing the sort of thrill she'd had when Pat's body had been on top of hers? Mmmmm...and what would it have been like if...if...Shelagh suppressed a giggle. She'd have to take the plunge sometime...learn what it was like to go all the way with a man...arh...mmm.. The first time would be...well, traumatic, bound to be and well, rationally, it might be wiser...less traumatic...to trust oneself with an expert like Pat rather than a fumbler like Andrew. If only...

Shelagh tightened her lips. What on earth was she thinking of? Thrilling or not, Pat Pendle was expert because he was a...a philanderer! She choked on the word, but it was the right one. It was what he was...and worse! Not only had he sought to violate her body, he was planning to rape her beautiful Humps as well. Spoil them with beastly nuclear waste. Where would rare old red-speckled *Triturus cristatus* be then? Wiped out! Along with everything else. Maggie was right. Pat Pendle was a prime example of all that was bad in a man...a womaniser ready to desecrate anybody and everything for his own selfish ends. He was beneath contempt...he had cried aloud that he loved her...but no, no, no...that had meant nothing. Love to him was a ploy, that's all, the final card in the seducer's game of sexual conquest. She never wanted to see him again...never! That was certain. Never...but where was he? Where had he gone? Damn him!

Pent-up Pat

He was in a cell in Brixton – trying to get that blasted Breagh girl out of his mind.

In London the police contented themselves with a bald announcement that a man had been charged for a breach of the Freedom of Information Act and bail had not been given. It was not long, however, before veiled hints began to appear in the more rarefied social publications about 'rural affairs', including humorous references to haycocks and rustic maidens. One satirical magazine reported that 'an expert on metropolitan affairs' had been caught revealing his secret methods to ignorant peasants, causing such outrage that he had been locked up for his own safety. It went on to claim that a number of public-spirited females had offered to take the offender into protective custody and provide him with intensive nursing at no cost to the public purse.

Pat heard little of this and cared less. He was past caring. He wanted only to get out and find somewhere to hide. The woman, blast her, had humiliated him...teased him...played with him...deliberately hiked him up the hill of expectation and dropped him from the summit. He hated her! Loathed her! But try as he might he could not shut the stupid woman from his mind. There seemed to be no escaping her. By day, remembrance of her obsessed him. At night, she possessed his dreams – tempting him to embrace her, pursuing him when he fled. It frightened him; he wanted to hide, to find somewhere safe from enslavement.

"Pricks!" says the Reverend

The Pendle family were outraged at Pat's imprisonment. Tom brought to bear all the power and influence of his wealth to secure his son's release, but to no avail.

"They tell us," said Bridget, expressing the opinion of their lawyers, "that the biggies want a pound of flesh and are determined to get it."

"Don't worry," said Paula Pomfrey. "Dad knows more about fixing things than any legal halfwit and he's not going to let anyone get at the Humps. He loves them. They're family history."

"But what can he do?"

"God knows! But I think he's up to something with Old Tom. They've been having a meeting, very hush-

hush."

"Surely the government can't do anything about the Humps now. There'd be too much of a fuss."

"Don't you believe it. They'll wait, bide their time, then start filling the hole when nobody's looking. That's what governments do, and it's what Dad's afraid of."

"But the people..." Bridget began.

"You don't know politicians, sweetheart," Paula squeezed her hand affectionately. "They hold grudges."

"Warwick certainly does," said Sylvia Tewson, squeezing Bridget's other hand. "He's lying low now but he'll get the Humps filled in somehow, just to spite us. He's as good as said so...the prick!"

Her companions laughed. They were amid the usual Sunday crowd slaking post-matins thirsts in the Beak and Wedge and Sylvia's description of her husband echoed the sermon they had just endured.

"Pricks!" the Reverend Breagh had valiantly proclaimed, entering the verbal maze that confronted him whenever he mounted the pulpit, "I take as my text, pricks. Acts of the Apostles, chapter nine, verse five. Pricks! Yes, pricks, brethren. We all know what pricks are! We have suffered many of late and like Saul before Damascus it is hard for us to kick against them − against the many government pricks that torment us − threatening to send destruction on us. Yet, as Joshua sang in thirteen, ten, is not this written in the book of Jasher? No, it cannot be!" he continued beginning to lose his way. "No! We are not Sodom or Gomorrah, no, we are not! We are being pricked because we have the Humps. But," he paused, fixing the congregation with his familiar accusing stare, "we cannot help having the Humps! It is unjust that we are being pricked for what are gifts of God...well," the demotic asserted itself, "one is anyway...so go in peace and pray for the end of our pricks with love and for salvation in the name of the Lord."

"You're rid of your prick now," said Paula, "or soon will be. We'll all be together then and..." She stopped and peered past the other two towards the bar. "There's Shelagh." Sylvia and Bridget twisted to look. "Shall I ask her to join us?"

"Too late," said Paula.

Shelagh was leaving the bar, thrusting her way through the crush towards the door. As she turned she spotted the three friends, waved, gave a wan smile and went out.

"She wasn't in church," said Bridget.

"I haven't seen her around much at all lately," said Sylvia. "Spends all her time with her warty newts. I'm sure it can't be good for her."

"She does look decidedly peaked," said Paula.

Trouble up the Humps

Mrs Breagh also thought her daughter looked peaked. "It's no good mooning about," she said. "Why not give Andrew a call? I'm sure he..."

"I'm not interested in Andrew," said Shelagh irritably. "And he is not interested in me."

"When I gave him the ring he..."

"Mother, please! Will you shut up about him?"

"Very well," said Mrs Breagh tightly, increasing her plaining and purling rate considerably. "If a mother can't talk to her daughter I suppose there is nothing to do but not. When you are a mother yourself maybe..."

"I shall never be a mother. There are too many children in the world as it is."

"Don't be silly. You have to do something. You're a woman."

"I shall take Orders."

"What!"

The Reverend Breagh had been deep in Revelations, it having occurred to him that the pollution of the Humps signalled the Pouring Out of the Seven Plagues from the Seven Bowls on an impenitent world lost in worship of the Beast. His daughter's remark pierced his ears like an arrow. He sat up with a jerk.

"It seems the only worthwhile thing to do. Try and save the world by spreading the good word."

"Really," said Mrs Breagh. "You can't be a priest. Your father is one already."

"I have thought about it before as you know and now women are generally accepted I think..."

"It does not matter whether they are accepted or not," the Rector burst out with surprising vehemence. "It is a squabble over a dried-up well."

"Oh," said Mrs Breagh. "What well? Where?"

"We priests are anachronisms, aesthetically offensive and theologically unnecessary. We spend our time pleading for place and status in a society that really doesn't want us, which sees miracles, sacraments, blessings and consecrations as ignorance and superstition – and without recognition of our sacerdotal authority, what can a priest do that a lay person cannot? We're a sort of stopgap: someone to turn to when the police, doctors and social services have given up. That's all."

"I meant to tell you," said his wife placidly. "Betty Simmonds can't do the flower rota. She's going to art classes."

"Dear God!" The Rector slammed Revelations shut. "The church has spent two thousand years worshipping, praying and glorifying God and produced nothing more than a congregation of women worrying about the flower rota."

He got up and confronted Shelagh. "I entered the church prepared to give my life to God. I was ready for martyrdom at the stake and I have ended up in a cage with the old, the sick and the garrulous. I sit through endless meetings of Scouts, Brownies, Women's Institutes, mothers' circles and a ragbag of the lonely, the senile and gossipy. I organise services to bless cats and dogs and wander round in circles trying to find my place in the world. Where do I fit in? I don't know. Boredom is my martyrdom. It is all there is on offer in the church today. Even for a woman."

"Oh Daddy," said Shelagh, moved. "You do a lot of good. You do. You mustn't think you've wasted your life."

He kissed her and smiled. "Wasted or not," he said, "it has taught me that we make our own heaven. It is inside us...where God is."

"I don't know what you mean, 'even for a woman'," said Mrs Breagh tartly.

"What I meant was – " said the Rector, and stopped in mid-sentence. "What's happening on the Humps?"

Shelagh turned. On the near horizon the night was split by dozens of moving lights. When the Rector opened the window the distant sounds of heavy engines could be heard, and almost simultaneously the church bells began to ring.

"They can't be starting the in-fill now, can they?" said Shelagh. "Not at this time of night."

"Maybe they've heard of the Action Group's plans and are trying to pre-empt them," said the Rector.

Shelagh made for the door. "Are you coming?"

"You go ahead. I must telephone Sir Archibald."

Shelagh went out hurriedly.

Mrs Breagh looked up from her knitting. "Where's Shelagh going, and why are the bells ringing?"

"They're saying farewell to the view," said her husband and reached for the telephone.

Witness

The only vehicle approach to the Humps was along a steeply rising dirt path leading off a lane half a mile or so outside the village. Shelagh arrived to find it jammed with emptying cars. People leaving them were racing along the gap at the side of the lane shouting and asking questions. No one seemed to know exactly what was happening but a giant yellow truck was lodged in the gap between the hedges that joined the dirt path to the lane. Around the rear of the truck a milling, shouting crowd was forming, and beyond it a long line of similar trucks stretched nose to tail, engines running, lights blazing, all the way up to the Humps. The din was terrific. If the infill had started, any chance of preventing it seemed doomed to failure.

In the glare of lights from the parked cars a man was climbing onto the back of one of the trucks. It was Ackers!

Once atop the truck he made a vain attempt to speak but was shouted down. Someone handed him a loudhailer and his voice boomed out over the clamour.

"Shut up, you stupid buggers," he yelled. "This isn't the infill...this isn't any nuclear stuff...it's...listen, will you hear me, you buggers...will you shut up and listen! This isn't nuclear waste...it's concrete!"

The announcement caused a stir, the crowd fell silent. Ackers reduced the volume on the loudhailer.

"I dunno who started the bells," he shouted more quietly, "but I suppose as everyone was expecting trouble this looked like it was it, but it ain't! You got a benefactor. Yes, you have but no names, no pack-drill. He's anonymous and staying it, and what he's doing is dumping a few hundred tons of concrete to block up the hole so it won't be easy for anyone to get anything else in without a lot of trouble and believe me..."

Whatever else Ackers wanted believed was lost in a

wild outburst of cheering. He paused a while then brought them to near silence again with a blast from the loudhailer.

"Shurrup again, shurrup, shurrup I said! Listen...listen...get out of the way and let the trucks get on with...get out the front of them...they're on our side you stupid buggers...don't you hear me? Get orf...we don't want any accidents...gerrorf, you wanna get run over?"

The message finally got through. People shouted to each other to get clear of the trucks. Ackers scrambled down and within minutes the way up to the Humps was cleared and the trucks began to roll. The crowd surged alongside, cheering and waving.

Shelagh stood silent. Ackers came up beside her and together they watched trucks and humans streaming uphill.

"What breaks my bloody heart", said Ackers, "is being glad to do down the bastards in the government at the same time as helping this load of hypocrites save their back yard. Enough to make you sick, enit?"

"Ackers," said Shelagh, "who's doing this?"

"Heard me, didn't you? It's anonymous. A secret."

"Is it Sir Archibald?"

"I'm saying nothing. Don't want to end up like your pal, do I?"

Shelagh experienced a slight frisson in her bowels. "My pal?"

"Him who had Pippit, you know. I'm sorry for him – was inside myself once for a bit of poaching and it ain't like home, I can tell you, but there always has to be a victim. I know cos I come from the class they pick 'em from...hey, hey, listen to them bells. I'd better get 'em stopped or we'll have the army here."

Ackers started off. Shelagh stopped him.

"Are you telling me that Pat Pendle is in prison?"

"So I have heard."

"But...but what for?"

"Opened up to you about this infilling lark, broke that Freedom Act nonsense, din he? Bureaucrats always get their man, so they got him. Bastards! And I gotta do those bells or someone else'll cop it."

Ackers went. Shelagh remained standing. The lights still blazed on the Humps, criss-crossing like searchlights. The shouting continued, more distant now but Shelagh hardly noticed. She was thinking of Pat. Imprisoned! And oh God! It was all her fault...her fault. It was...it was! No! No, it wasn't! Never! He was getting what he deserved...she had no pity for him. None! But...well, as a Christian she...no, no! No one who was prepared to ruin the Humps for profit deserved pity or help or forgiveness! Don't think of it! Forget him...he wasn't worth...

"Shelagh! Are you all right?" Andrew Hawkins was at her shoulder. "You look sort of like you've had a shock."

"Is it true Pat Pendle's in prison?"

"Didn't you know?"

"Of course I didn't," said Shelagh impatiently. "Ackers has only just told me."

"Oh, I see, well they wouldn't give him bail, quite right too. I'm being called as a witness, aren't you?"

"Witness of what?"

"Of what happened – of how he let the cat out of the bag about the Humps after I stopped him trying to rape you."

"He wasn't trying to rape me!" Shelagh said indignantly. Andrew laughed. "He wanted to make love to me, that's all!" Andrew laughed again. Shelagh boiled over. "It was my fault. I tempted him. I knew what he wanted and was leading him on."

"Don't be silly," said Andrew. "You couldn't lead a man on if you tried."

"I could and I did."

"He was trying to rape you."

"He was not... I was leading him and he..."

"For God's sake!" Andrew interrupted her, suddenly impatient. "You're scared of sex, you wouldn't let a man get past your kneecap."

"The right man I would," said Shelagh. "One who knew how to go about it."

"I see," said Andrew stiffly. "Well I'm sorry I spoiled your enjoyment of his expertise." He turned away.

Shelagh overcome with remorse caught his arm. "I'm sorry, Andrew... I am...but...I love him."

"You're mad," said Andrew briefly.

"I can't help it... I don't want to love him but I just do."

"Then for your sake I shall do all I can to get him jailed for life."

"Andrew, please..."

"He was trying to rape you, and in court I shall tell them just that."

"No, Andrew, you mustn't."

"Try and stop me," he said and strode off up the Humps.

Virgin Decisive

Shelagh wandered back to the Rectory in a state of panic, convinced that she had ruined Pat Pendle's life. He would be a convicted criminal, a jailbird, because she had caused him to break some silly Act and...oh my God! She almost swooned on the spot. If they believed Andrew, the man she loved would be convicted of raping her – labelled a rapist! Andrew was mistaken...Pat hadn't...wasn't...it was all her fault. She had to do something...she had to save Pat. She loved him. Yes, she did, she did...dear heaven! She'd been a fool, a stupid utter virginal fool. He had faults, of course, she wasn't going to let love make her blind to that. No! No, never! But she could live with them, and once they were married...married? Yes married! Of course they had to be...oh grief, she went weak at the knees...yes, but first she had to save him. How? How? How? HOW?

The question beat at her brain and she was back in the village before, as if by magic, the fog of uncertainty cleared. The solution was obvious! If Andrew was going to be a witness at the trial she'd be one too. Of course! And if they believed Pat was trying to rape her she'd tell them she liked her sex that way as it was more exciting! And she'd make them believe it too.

At the Rectory a small party clustered round the picture window looking across Pitts' field to the Humps, the lights of the trucks still visible at the top of the lane. Sir Archibald Pomfrey, her parents and the local action committee were celebrating victory. Shelagh, in no mood for partying, immediately tried to retreat but Sylvia Tewson stopped her.

"Great, isn't it?" said the MP's wife. "Even my near ex says nuclear waste on the Humps will be a dead duck now so your newts are safe too." She nodded to the group at the window. "Nobody knows quite who's responsible but the betting is that Sir Archy had more than a hand in it."

"We Pomfreys have a hand in everything," said Paula, coming to them with Bridget. "With Shelagh we'd be a nice cosy foursome. Why not ask her to join us, Sylv?"

Sylvia reddened slightly. "We're talking about waste, Paula."

"It is a waste. We know you like Shelagh so why not ask..."

"Nuclear waste!" Sylvia put in quickly to cover her embarrassment. "It was the government who chose where to dump, not Mr Pendle. Isn't that right, Bridget?"

"I never choose anything," said Bridget, smiling at

Paula, "I wait to be chosen."

Paula laughed, putting her arm round Sylvia. "We've chosen each other," she said, and winked at Shelagh. "Why not join us?"

The invitation could hardly have been clearer, but the sex on Shelagh's mind was of a different nature. Bridget was Pat's sister – if anyone had news of him, she would.

"I hear your brother's been arrested," she said, trying, not very successfully, to keep her voice calm. "How is he?"

Bridget giggled. "I'm told he's all right but I haven't seen him. He's not allowed visitors," she said and added, almost in apology, "Paula's Dad has got all sorts of lawyers working on it, and he's told us not to worry."

"But is it...will it...could he get a long sentence?"

"No one has the faintest idea," said Paula, "it depends on the judge, but we'll know soon enough – the trial's on Thursday."

Tears came to Shelagh's eyes. Her feelings were confused, but one thing was clear in her mind. It was all very well being told not to worry but if anyone could save Pat she could by volunteering as a witness and confounding Andrew's evidence. It meant she had to get to London as quickly as possible. Her mind made up she ran for the door. The others looked at each other blankly.

"I think she has a thing about Pat," said Sylvia.

"Then God help her," said Bridget. "He'll have her, but she'll never get him."

Virgin Determined

The receptionist in the marbled entrance lobby of Pendle's Disposal plc's massive London HQ told Shelagh that Mr Tom Pendle was not in the office at present and no, she couldn't give anyone his private address. It wasn't allowed.

In desperation Shelagh phoned Stoke Kirby to ask Bridget. It was answered by Paula who told her the address at once, then asked with a throaty chuckle if she was hoping to see Pat. There was no point in denying it so Shelagh agreed she was.

"Tut, tut," said Paula, "you're too beautiful to be wasted on a man. Join us."

"Thank you but no."

"Well, remember, you can call me any time. I'm always available," said Paula and rang off, leaving Shelagh to wonder if Sylvia Tewson realised what she had let herself in for.

Virgin *En Famille*

The street the cab turned into was lined with cars parked nose to tail before late Victorian semi-detached houses, hardly an area where one would expect a multi-millionaire to live. Only when the driver stopped by a pair of green double gates decorated with the legend 'PENDLE'S WASTE DISPOSAL' was Shelagh convinced that he'd got the address right.

She left the cab and stood looking at the lace-curtained, bay-windowed house alongside the gates. On the front door a white, enamelled plaque decorated with bluebells announced that she was standing before 'Bluebell Cottage'.

Shelagh paused a long moment before opening the scrolled iron gate and crossing the narrow enclosed concrete area to the front door. She had taken it for granted that all the Pendles were sophisticated urbanites like Pat and Bridget, worldly people to whom one could talk of sex without embarrassment. Her plan had been to tell them frankly of exactly how their son had come to violate the Freedom of Information Act and, at the same time, clear him of any allegation of rape.

Confronted by Bluebell Cottage's aura of old-fashioned, cockney respectability, confidence in her plan wilted. When Dolly Pendle opened the door in response to the syncopated chimes of the doorbell it vanished completely!

How could she possibly tell this rolled-up dumpling of a woman in a flowered wraparound overall that her son had...oh dear God! Shelagh blushed at the thought of describing Pat trying to remove her knickers in an ecstasy of sexual excitement.

"Hello," said the flowered dumpling, smiling. "What can I do for you?"

"Er," said Shelagh, hesitating. "It's about Pat. I..."

"Pat? Pat? My son Pat?" The smile vanished, replaced by a look of alarm. "What's happened now?"

"No, no, it's nothing new," said Shelagh hurriedly. "It's just that I know he's in prison and I'm a friend of his and I wanted to, well...it's difficult to explain and..."

She trailed off, unsure how to proceed. She need not have worried. Dolly proceeded for her.

"A friend! Oh come in then, come in." She held wide the door, closed it and bustled Shelagh into the front room, talking all the time. "Any friend of Pat's is welcome. Very welcome. Come on in...it's dreadful, isn't it? Come on in. Now you sit here while I make a cup of tea and get Mr Pendle and... You're comfy there, are you?"

"Yes, thank you. I want to...I mean, I think I can help Pat and I…"

"You do? Oh, that is kind. Now you sit comfy there while I get Mr Pendle and you can tell him. Won't be a sec and we'll have a nice cup too. Oh dear!"

Mrs Pendle bustled breathlessly out and burst even more breathlessly into the bedroom where her husband was halfway into a low-cut, salmon-pink fifties ball gown he'd bought at the local Oxfam shop.

"Tom! Tom!" she panted. "There's a woman here says she can help Pat."

"What?"

"I'll get the kettle on. You come down quick."

"Hang on, hang on! Who is she? Do we know her?"

Halfway out of the door, Dolly stopped. "I don't."

"If you don't, I won't. So how can she help Pat?"

"I don't know, you'll have to ask her. Lucky I got some cup cakes from Yorick's, and that pink doesn't suit you, Tom."

"I like it."

"That's no excuse and hurry up. Please!"

She was gone before he could tell her that what he liked was his business and she wouldn't be wearing it.

When he got to the front room Shelagh was alone. She got to her feet as he entered.

"Ah, um," he said, surprised. "Where's the missus?"

"Making tea, I think."

"Oh ay, and you're a friend of Pat's, are you?"

Without waiting for an answer Tom held out his hand Shelagh offered hers and it disappeared in the old man's colossal fist. "I'm his Dad. Who are you?"

The old man's face was familiar, but she couldn't place it. "I'm Shelagh Breagh and I..."

"The missus tells me you can help Pat."

"I hope so. I..."

"Well I can't say he doesn't need some. Sit down then and tell me what you can do."

"I...er...well..."

Unnerved by the old man's blunt approach Shelagh hesitated. Sex was definitely off the conversational agenda. She searched her mind for inspiration.

"Well, what?"

Inspiration came. "Pat didn't mean to say anything

about the dumping on the Humps. It wasn't intentional. I can tell the court that."

"You were with him when he said it then?"

She nodded. "Oh yes."

"What were you doing?"

Shelagh gulped, a vision of wrestling with Pat flashing across her mind.

"I was...I was...we were...er, together...in a cottage and...he just said it."

"Why? What's he want to say it for? He must have had a reason."

"He...he...er..." Shelagh paused. The old man's eyes were fixed on her, demanding an answer. "He'd...it was the man who was with us...they'd had a...a...row over something."

Tom kept his eyes on her. Shelagh stared back disconcerted; if he asked her what the 'something' was what could she say?!

But her hesitancy gave Old Tom an uneasy feeling that the 'something' was sex and sex was a subject he was incapable of discussing freely with his wife let alone a modern young woman.

They were still silent, eyes fixed on each other in a conversational impasse, when Dolly arrived with tea and cakes, neatly arranged on the chrome and imitation gold trolley she'd got in exchange for two and a half thousand loyalty coupons at a nearby supermarket.

"Do you want milk, dear?" she asked cheerfully, sitting next to Shelagh. "And do have a cup cake. They're Yorick's and Tom loves them, don't you, Tom?"

Tom took no notice. Sir Archibald had advised him to leave everything to the law firm he had recommended, and Dolly's arrival settled his mind. Sir Archy was right! Even more so now there was a woman, and maybe sex, to be sorted out. Lawyers had no shame. Let them handle it.

"I'll have a word with Mr Mishon who's doing Pat's defence," he said to Shelagh, "and arrange for you to meet him at the court tomorrow before the trial starts. Will that suit you?"

"Oh yes. Yes, please," said Shelagh, relieved beyond measure.

"I'll telephone him then."

Tom left the room.

"Do have a cup cake," said Dolly. "They're Yorick's. Lovely. Now do tell me how you get on with Pat. He's a lovely boy, isn't he, don't you think?"

Virgin still Determined

Shelagh spent the night with her oldest friend but received neither sympathy for her feelings nor approval of her plan, only advice she didn't want to hear.

"I warned you, didn't I? The man is poison, a menace. Go home and forget him."

"But he's innocent."

"There is no such thing as an innocent man."

"You're prejudiced. He's innocent and I must do something."

"I am prejudiced," said Maggie Williams firmly. "Do nothing, don't lift a finger."

"He's in prison and might be kept there."

"Let's hope he is. The longer he is, the safer you'll be."

"I don't want to be safe."

Maggie gave a frightened squawk. "Emigrate, enter a convent, do good works, help the aged, walk the Pilgrims' Way. Do anything but don't go..."

"I love him, Maggie."

"What!"

"I love him."

"See a psychiatrist."

"But..."

"At once! Go straight out and get yourself seen to... I'll take you."

"I want to marry him."

Maggie's jaw dropped. She gazed at her friend, unbelievingly, speechless.

"I know he's got faults," said Shelagh tremulously, "but so have I, so have we all, don't you think?"

"I think," said Maggie, having trouble finding her voice, "you're absolutely and completely nuts."

"I don't care, I do love him and I think he loves me."

"Oh my God! Don't tell me...don't. Please! I don't want to know."

"I want everyone to know. I want to tell the world."

"Then do it...go and shout it out to anyone who'll listen."

"Oh, Maggie, do you mean that?"

"I most certainly do! They'll know at once that you are mentally up the Orinoco and put you away."

He's the King of the One-night Stands

Maggie drove her to court the next day still bitterly accusing her of treason to their sex but Shelagh was unmoved. She'd spent some time deciding on a form of dress likely to impress the judge and ameliorate the sexual details of her evidence. Not having packed much she'd bought a simple white cotton dress at C&A that gave her an aura of innocent vulnerability, but also displayed to perfection the attractions of her feminine figure. To emphasise the effect of virginal innocence she added a chiffon scarf of daffodil yellow about her neck and the faintest wisp of pale cerise to her lips.

The end product was a vision of unsullied maidenhood: the epitome of every man's desire capable, she reasoned guiltily but hopefully (for such a deliberate attempt at male tempting was alien to her nature), of evoking sympathy from the most hard-hearted judge.

The Pendle family were with a thin, grey-faced man in wig and gown at the bottom of the short flight of broad steps leading to the court in which Pat was to face trial.

They greeted her gloomily. Mr Mishon QC, allegedly one of best defence lawyers in the land, was as pessimistic as his countenance. Learning that Shelagh was ready to contradict anything the prosecution witness might say (she was careful not to hint about what) and sustain a plea that Pat's breach of the Freedom of Information Act was unintentional, blurted out unthinkingly, did nothing to lighten his despondency. The prosecution's witness, he pointed out, might have quite a different opinion of the accused's intentions. Nevertheless it might be helpful. He would see what could be done.

"I will plead for you to be heard," he said, "but at this late stage the judge will decide whether you can be called, and the prosecution is sure to object. I am not a pessimist," he continued, before proceeding to disprove his words, "but the fact is they've got us over a barrel. They don't have to define national or public safety as it's secret and Mr Pendle spoke out of turn in class, and is very likely to cop it. We can't even appeal for public sympathy because the media's gagged too. We are back in the Middle Ages, I'm afraid, but I'll do my best."

Having thus comforted the family, he made to leave. Shelagh stopped him.

"Can I come in and see him?"

"No...no, impossible. The hearing is in camera."

"Can you give Pat a letter for me then?"

The eminent QC pondered the request before answering. "He's not convicted yet so yes...yes. I think I can do that."

Shelagh handed him a letter. He accepted it with the ghost of a smile. "Don't give up hope," he said, and left.

"Gawd," said Tim to his father as the lawyer departed. "He's a ray of sunshine. Where did you find him?"

"Sir Archy said he was the best."

Bridget said to Shelagh, "Paula sends her love, so does Sylv."

"Thank you, but I'm more concerned about your brother, as I think you should be."

"I am," Bridget, put an arm round Shelagh's shoulder, "but I am also concerned about you. He's got you wanting him, hasn't he?"

"I love him."

"Don't! He'll never love you. As far as women are concerned he is – forgive me you won't like this – but the fact is my lovely brother is king of the one-night stands! In plain English he's a marauding, feckless, faithless fucker. A no-good for women."

Shelagh stared at her, white, tight-lipped. Bridget was moved to pity. "I'm sorry, duckie," she added. "That's the truth and nothing but the truth. Take my advice – run and keep running. You're too good to be wasted on him."

Shelagh was unmoved. They all misunderstood Pat. She knew what he was really like – underneath.

Ill at ease with officialdom of any kind Dolly had not uttered a word since entering the building: she was there only because it was where she knew she had to be. With the family – supporting them. Bewildered and uncomfortable on one of the benches lining the corridor her eyes were on Shelagh. Over the cup cakes and tea of the previous night she had persuaded herself that the nice-looking country girl would be a nice addition to the family – as Pat's wife.

The Threatening Letter

Mr Mishon, visiting Pat while waiting for their case to be called, told him that the crown prosecutor Sir David Laney – an old friend, he was careful to explain – had raised no objection to a new witness for the defence and the judge had agreed. It would probably make no difference to the verdict but if she spoke well of him the judge might look favourably on a non-custodial sentence.

"She?" Pat questioned. "Who?"

"Her name is Shelagh Breagh. I presume you know her."

"Oh my God!" said Pat.

"She seems a very pleasant young woman and I have... Oh, she gave me this for you."

Mr Mishon produced Shelagh's letter. Pat stared at it dumbly, his stomach beginning to quake.

"You better read it before I go; we don't want any surprise revelations the prosecution could pounce on." Mr Mishon looked at his watch. "We do not have a lot of time."

Pat took the letter and opened it, his hand shaking.

'Dear Pat,' he read. 'I want to say how sorry I am for the way I behaved when you tried to seduce me. After all, it is quite natural for you, a man, to try and have your way with me, a woman. Nature wants us to do it, and more and more we are beginning to realise how important it is to cooperate with nature. That does not mean that I have to let you do it if I don't want you to, but I think I do. Really. Anyway we can talk about it when you are free, which I am sure you will be when I tell them you only said about the waste because you were angry after Andrew punched you because it looked like you were raping me when really I had tempted you to frustration. Please don't despair. I'm sure that if we are open and honest about everything the judge will understand that you were too worked up to know what you were doing. I love you.'

It was signed Shelagh.

Pat put his head in his hands. She was going into the witness box to tell...oh Jesus. No! She was going to humiliate him...secret hearing or not it would get out. He'd end up a laughing stock of every club in London...and the family. Oh Christ! Why did he ever go near the bloody woman!

Mr Mishon was eyeing him curiously. "Is anything the matter, Mr Pendle?"

"Everything's the bloody matter," Pat burst out unable to contain himself. "I'm not...I don't...I don't want her as a witness, understand? You're not to call her. I won't have her as a witness. Send her away."

"I'm afraid that's impossible," said Mr Mishon, stiffly. He had gone to a lot of trouble to get the new witness admitted and expected thanks, not rejection. "She is on the list to appear."

"Never mind the list. You don't have to call her."

"If I don't it will invite suspicion, surely even you can

see that."

"I don't care what they suspect – I don't want her called."

"Your wants won't count. If I don't call her Sir David most certainly will if only to find out why I haven't." Mr Mishon spoke feelingly. Late withdrawal of a witness after pleading late admission would make him look foolish. "He will suspect from your attitude, as I do, that she may reveal matters you prefer to keep hidden."

"Jesus," his client groaned desperately. "How do I get out of this!"

"It will help if you tell me what you are afraid the witness might disclose. I can then prepare for anything a hostile cross-examination may bring to light."

"I don't want her cross-examined!"

"I'm afraid that cannot be avoided. Sir David will call..."

"I'd rather plead guilty."

"I cannot see..."

"Guilty...yes, I'll plead guilty."

Mr Mishon was shocked. "Do you want to go to prison?"

"That's it, yes. Yes, I do!"

Pat suddenly brightened; it was the brightness of desperation but it solved problems: by pleading guilty he would avoid Shelagh's and Andrew's...Jesus he'd forgotten Andrew and what he might say! Gawd...his inside shrivelled at the thought. Better incarceration than humiliation and – a bonus not be sneezed at – he'd be taken from court in a black maria and locked up – safely out of Shelagh's reach.

"Guilty," he said. "I'm pleading guilty and I want a long sentence."

"But Mr Pendle, you..."

"Life will do nicely."

"But..."

"No buts, no arguments. I'm pleading guilty."

Mr Mishon opened his mouth to renew his protest, and was told not to waste his breath. Outside the Rector's daughter lurked, waiting...waiting to ensnare him. If she got close, no, no, not even close: if he only caught sight of her...just one glance and he'd weaken...he knew it...he would...he'd weaken and she'd nab him – for keeps.

Prison was a place of salvation. Prison meant safety. God bless prison!

Mr Mishon left the cell bemused and bewildered to seek out Sir Archibald Pomfrey who was waiting in an anteroom to the judge's chambers. He caught him just before the judge left to open the trial.

The Judge Delivers

"Members of the jury, the defendant has changed his plea to guilty," Judge Killearn leaned forward, tweaking a pencil between his fingers. "I accept his plea, so you have no case to decide. However, before I pass sentence and discharge you from your duty, I wish to make this clear. British justice is famed throughout the world for its impartiality and independence. This reputation derives, in part, from its openness. It hides nothing – except of course when the government in its wisdom decides otherwise." He paused. "As in this case it has. You have all been sworn to secrecy because the government believes that if the facts of this case were generally known they would constitute a threat to national security and public order." He paused again. "What are the facts? They are these: the government has plans to dump nuclear waste on a habitat of the great horned newt, an area of beauty known as the Humps. This secret plan became known to the citizens of Longford Stanton who, understandably, were not pleased.

When it later became known that the local member of parliament, who is the Minister for Rural Affairs and lives locally, was trying to sell his house before nuclear dumping started, their displeasure turned to anger: indeed so angry were they that they put the minister in the stocks – a medieval contraption wherein offenders are imprisoned by their arms and legs – and pelted him with decaying vegetable matter and, particularly, eggs." Judge Killearn barely suppressed a smile. "You may sympathise with the minister. It must have been an unhappy experience for him, albeit apt punishment for the exercise of not untypical political self-interest and greed; you may also conclude that if plans are afoot to put people in situations of danger and financial loss they have a right to know about them." Judge Killearn paused, and inspected the back of his hands before continuing. "This case is here because the government in its wisdom has decided that they do not have that right. It appears to believe that keeping the public in ignorance helps national security and public order. In reality, of course, it is to avoid awkward questions about the validity and worth of particular policies. But we are not here to protect the government. Our task is to observe the law and administer justice. Had the defendant not pleaded guilty the verdict would have been in your hands. In summing up I would have pointed out that the only way the defendant could warn people of a danger to their lives and properties was by breaking the law. You would have had to decide whether he should be punished for this." The judge scanned the jury so as to look each individual in the eye. "I don't think he should. I think he should be congratulated."

The jury started to applaud. Judge Killearn smiled and lifted his hand for silence.

"I am glad you agree. Of course the law is the law and no one should escape it, but it is my opinion that the

Freedom of Information Act is ambiguously worded, drafted quite deliberately to provide a hiding place for timid politicians who do not have the courage of their electors' convictions. It has deprived the word Freedom of any meaning."

Again the jurors clapped. Again he stopped them and smiled, this time at Pat Pendle who stood in the dock as baffled as the clerks and lawyers around him.

"You have pleaded guilty," said Judge Killearn, "so I am bound to pass sentence. But this is my last appearance in court and I am not going to end my legal career by punishing a man indicted under a stupid and undemocratic law. Patrick Pendle, I sentence you to whatever time you have served while awaiting trial. You are therefore free to go. Free, may I add, to kiss the beautiful girl who is waiting for you outside."

The jury applauded vigorously. Pat stood petrified!

Freedom! Where? Outside an enchantress waited with one ring for her finger and another for his nose. The blast of the wedding march filled the courtroom. 'Wilt thou' and 'I will' echoed in his head. A vision of the shared slavery of home and habit flashed before him and – oh dear God – the patter of little feet and sleepless nights! Panic immobilised him.

Moved to wonder by Pat's seeming paralysis the applause faltered and stopped.

"Mr Pendle," said Judge Killearn, "did you hear me? You are free to go."

Pat turned and stumbled from the dock, ignoring the renewed applause and hands outstretched in congratulation. A warder took him by the elbow, slapped him on the back and pushed him through the courtroom door.

Halfway down the steps Old Tom, Dolly, Tim and Bridget were coming up to meet him. Behind them standing like a statue at the bottom, her lips trembling, was the enchantress. With a yelp of anguish Pat bolted back into the courtroom, slamming the door behind him.

"It's that way out," said the warder.

"Not for me," said Pat. "Anyway but that way."

"Oh, family, is it?" said the warder. "I know how you feel. Hey, Augustus." He beckoned his companion. "Mr Pendle don't want to meet his missus. Show him the back way."

Augustus led Pat through a maze of corridors to the staff entrance, which gave onto a narrow deserted street. He was halfway up this when he realised it would take him round to the front of the court. As he turned back a taxi came round the corner and stopped beside him. He jumped in, gave a cry of alarm and tried to get out again but Shelagh grabbed his arm, pulled him onto the seat and flung her arms round his neck.

"Oh Pat," she cried. "Oh Pat, isn't it wonderful? You're free. Free."

Unable to resist Pat Pendle's arm went around her.

Out of the Strong comes forth Something

"Do you," intoned the Reverend Breagh, "Patrick Thomas Pendle, take this woman, Shelagh Theresa Breagh, to be your lawful wedded wife?"

Pat hesitated. Shelagh squeezed his hand and his nerve failed him. He capitulated.

"I do," he said.

Mrs Breagh smirked at Mrs Hawkins who smiled condescendingly back. Andrew stared at the bride's back. Bridget, Paula and Sylvia clasped hands tightly. Tim and his partner exchanged smiles, Dolly gave Old Tom such a hugely delightful one that he edged away uneasily, afraid she was about to embrace him in public.

Mounting the pulpit, the bride's father swept the

congregation with a benevolent eye and proclaimed the theme of his homily. "If thou hadst not ploughed with my heifer, ye had not solved my riddle," he began, and paused impressively. "Riddle brethren! Whose riddle? Whose heifer? Who ploughed and, perhaps more importantly, who riddled, and why? And what you may well ask, have riddles and ploughing heifers to do with matrimony? Judges fourteen, fifteen." The Rector paused again, as if savouring the bafflement of his hearers. "The good book tells us. Out of the eater came forth meat and out of the strong sweetness! That is the riddle, and love is the answer. Yes love, brethren; in love Samson posed the riddle – and it was out of love for her family that his wife gave them the answer he had given her because he loved her. Naturally, as well as loving her, Samson was annoyed as he had to give them thirty garments for knowing it. Judges fourteen, thirteen to nineteen. But I say to you," he looked on the happy pair who gazed back glassy-eyed, "we have to puzzle out like Samson that whatever bees and eaten lions and sweetness may do, Judges thirteen, fourteen, as I have remarked, we can love and be annoyed at the same time. Remember this," his glance moved to Mrs Breagh, "it is love that overcomes the irritations that sometimes cloud wedlock. Patience is needed! Yes patience, and a lot of it and...er...on both...by both partners. Remember He that is Mighty hath done great things today. He has brought these two young people together in holy wedlock so we all need to pray. Therefore let us pray – particularly for them. May the Lord bless them and show them where the honey is. Amen."

As they left the church Judge Killearn said, "If I remember rightly Samson was so annoyed with his wife that he gave her away to his companion."

"He'd never have managed that if his wife had been Shelagh," said Sir Archy.

EPILOGUE

Peace Abroad

Sir Archibald shifted in his seat and eased his feet onto a stool.

"Of course I applaud the creation of a Minister of Consumer Care," he said. "But to put a man like Tewson in charge! Good heavens, it defeats the whole idea."

"I dare say that is the idea," said Killearn. He blew out a stream of cigar smoke and watched it rise upwards in the still, Tuscan air. "Much as it was when he had Rural Affairs. With the present PM, ineffectiveness is often a virtue."

They were enjoying the late afternoon sun on a patio that looked down on a valley with vines and olive trees. Children were playing between them and their shouts and calls could be heard distantly.

The old men sat in silence for a while, Sir Archibald gazing at a letter he was holding.

"Shall we go to Tom Pendle's presentation?" he said eventually.

"What's he going to call himself?"

"Baron Pendle of the Humps, I expect."

The judge chuckled appreciatively.

"Paula says she could fit us in at Stoke Kirby, though God knows where. Since Sylvia joined them the place seems to be always full of women." Sir Archibald consulted the letter again. "She says the young Pendles want you to be godfather to the twins. They're going to write."

"Hmmm. Do you think I should?"

"Why not?"

The judge gazed down the valley. "I'm not sure I believe in God," he said. "But I do believe in guilt. And I feel shamed."

"Don't follow you. Shamed of what?"

"Those children there." The judge nodded down the valley. "I could go and speak to them. They would have no fear. In England they would run away. Like we have."

"You mean we should go back?"

"Certainly not," said the judge. "Did not the Lord say that one had to be like children to get to heaven?"

THE END